"You can't want to marry me. I'm not a blue-blooded Spanish woman, and I wouldn't know how to be a *duquesa*."

"It's true you are not an ideal choice," Ramon

CHANTELLE SHAW lives on the Kent coast, five minutes from the sea, and does much of her thinking about the characters in her books while walking on the beach. An avid reader from an early age, she found that school friends used to hide their books when she visited, but Chantelle would retreat into her own world, and still writes stories in her head all the time. Chantelle has been blissfully married to her own tall, dark and very patient hero for more than twenty years and has six children. She began to read Harlequin® romances as a teenager, and throughout the years of being a stay-at-home mom to her brood, found romantic fiction helped her to stay sane! Her aim is to write books that provide an element of escapism, fun and of course romance for the countless women who juggle work and a home life and who need their precious moments of "me" time. She enjoys reading and writing about strong-willed, feisty women and even stronger-willed, sexy heroes. Chantelle is at her happiest when writing. She is particularly inspired while cooking dinner, which unfortunately results in a lot of culinary disasters! She also loves gardening, taking her very badly behaved terrier for walks and eating chocolate (followed by more walking—at least the dog is slim!).

HIS UNKNOWN HEIR

CHANTELLE SHAW

~ Aristocrats' Reluctant Brides ~

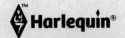

Harlequin®

TORONTO NEW YORK LONDON
AMSTERDAM PARIS SYDNEY HAMBURG
STOCKHOLM ATHENS TOKYO MILAN MADRID
PRAGUE WARSAW BUDAPEST AUCKLAND

Recycling programs
for this product may
not exist in your area.

ISBN-13: 978-0-373-88193-2

HIS UNKNOWN HEIR

First North American Publication 2011

Copyright © 2011 by Chantelle Shaw

This edition published by arrangement with Harlequin Books S.A.

For questions and comments about the quality of this book
please contact us at Customer_eCare@Harlequin.ca.

® and TM are trademarks of the publisher. Trademarks indicated with
® are registered in the United States Patent and Trademark Office, the
Canadian Trade Marks Office and in other countries.

www.Harlequin.com

Printed in U.S.A.

HIS UNKNOWN HEIR

For my wonderful mother-in-law, Julia,
my other mum.

Thank you for all your encouragement.

PROLOGUE

RAMON VELAQUEZ'S private jet touched down at London City Airport exactly on schedule. He swiftly cleared customs, and as he walked out of the airport building to his waiting limousine his chauffeur sprang forward to take his suitcase.

'Welcome back, Mr Velaquez. I hope you had a good trip.'

'*Gracias*, Paul.' Ramon climbed into the rear of the car and rested his dark head against the plush leather upholstery. A sense of well-being swept through him when he lifted the glass of whisky and soda that had been prepared for him from the drinks cabinet. 'It's good to be home.'

As the car pulled smoothly away he dwelled on his unconscious use of the word home. Because of course England was *not* his home; he was Spanish, and immensely proud of his country and his long and noble ancestry. His true home was the Castillo del Toro, and one day—he feared in the not too distant future, when he considered his father's health problems—he would be the new Duque de Velaquez and would live permanently at the castle, surrounded by an army of servants.

He knew from his childhood that it would be a life dictated by formality and protocol—so different from the relaxed atmosphere of his London penthouse apartment, where he employed the minimum of staff and enjoyed a sense of freedom away from the avid gaze of the Spanish media.

He felt a faint pang of guilt that he had chosen to fly from his business meeting in New York to England rather than to Spain. He cared deeply for his parents, but he had been reluctant to face another lecture about the necessity for him to marry a highborn Spanish woman and provide an heir to ensure the continuation of the illustrious family name. So he had made the excuse that he needed to be in London to deal with an urgent business matter.

Ramon knew his father, the Duque, was pleased with his dedication to Velaquez Conglomerates, but it was doubtful he would be so impressed if he knew that Ramon's real reason for racing back to London was because he was impatient to see his English mistress.

Lauren was at her desk, reading through a complicated lease agreement, when her mobile phone rang. Her heart gave a jolt, and she scrabbled in her handbag, a smile curving her lips when she saw that the caller was Ramon. She had been on tenterhooks all day, waiting for him to call. Like a lovesick teenager in the throes of her first romance, she thought ruefully.

Of course today there was a special reason why she was anxious to speak to him, she acknowledged, feeling once again the curious sensation that she was plummeting downwards in a fast-moving lift and had left her stomach behind. She was still reeling from the shock she had received a week ago—still couldn't quite believe it was true. It had made her desperate to hear Ramon's voice and to feel reassured that their relationship had developed into something deeper than a casual sexual liaison.

The closeness that she sensed had grown between them over the past months was not simply her imagination or wishful thinking, she assured herself. When she had first met the enigmatic Spaniard in a nightclub six months ago her journalist friend Amy had told her that Ramon Velaquez had a reputation as a playboy—but he conducted his affairs discreetly, and his love-life was rarely reported by the English media.

Lauren had been unable to deny the fierce chemistry that had blazed between her and Ramon, but mindful of Amy's warning, she had embarked on an affair with him accepting that he would not want a serious relationship any more than she did. She was busy with her career and sceptical of love. And yet somehow, against all the odds, a relationship had developed between them that she felt was more than simply mind-blowing sex.

Admittedly Ramon discouraged discussions about his personal life. All she really knew about him was that his family owned a famous winery in the Rioja region of Northern Spain. But in every other way they were a couple who shared a life together: companionship, laughter, a mutual appreciation of art galleries and the theatre, and frequently, of late, Ramon's London apartment. For whenever he was in town Lauren always stayed with him.

One important lesson she had learned during their affair was that he disliked displays of emotion, and an instinctive sense of self-protection had made her keep to herself the fact that she had fallen in love with him. But now she forgot her resolve to act cool with him, and quickly answered her phone.

The sound of his gravelly, sexy accent sent a little shiver of pleasure down her spine. '*Buenas tardes*, Lauren.'

'Ramon.' Her voice sounded annoyingly breathless, but she had never been able to control the effect he had on her. 'How was your trip?'

'Successful. You must know me well enough by now, *querida*, to understand that I would not settle for anything less.'

Ramon had smiled at the sound of Lauren's voice. It was good to be back in London, and even better to know that soon he would be making love to his beautiful English rose, whose demure smile hid a delightfully passionate nature.

Business had kept him in the States for two weeks, and he was impatient to relieve the ache of sexual frustration that had grown more intense with every day that he had been away. Lauren had been in his mind more often than he was comfortable with, but now was not the time to question why she had such an effect on him. He wanted her with an urgency he had never felt for any of his previous lovers, and he knew that tonight she would be gratifyingly impatient for him to take her to bed.

He almost gave in to the temptation to instruct her meet him at his apartment when she finished work, but he resisted. A leisurely meal in an exclusive restaurant would heighten his anticipation of the delights to follow, and on a practical level he had refused the bland in-flight meals served on the plane so it was not only his sexual appetite that demanded appeasement.

'I've booked a table at the Vine for seven-thirty,' he said. It was satisfying to reflect on his business trip, which had gone just the way he had planned it. As usual he had left nothing to chance, and the take-over bid had been completed with a brutal swiftness that had taken his competitors by surprise. 'We're celebrating.'

Lauren's heart missed a beat, and for a few seconds her brain went into freefall before her common sense returned. She was the only person in the world who knew the result of the pregnancy test she had done a week ago. There was no way Ramon could be suggesting that they were celebrating the fact that she was expecting his baby, which must mean—Lauren's heart gave another little flip—he had remembered it was the six-month anniversary of when they had first met.

She stared at the silk tie she had bought him after spending her entire lunch-break agonising over whether she should give him an anniversary gift. Clearly she had made the right decision. Ramon had remembered the special significance of today, and tonight, over dinner, she would tell him about the baby.

'Wonderful,' she murmured, unable to disguise the little tremor in her voice. Trying to hide her feelings for Ramon was always a struggle, and the knowledge that she was carrying his child made it even harder to mask her emotions.

Ramon glanced at his watch. 'I'll meet you at the restaurant in three hours.'

A little shiver of pleasure ran through Lauren at the thought of seeing him again, but she could not help feeling anxious at the prospect of telling him about the baby. 'I can't wait to see you,' she said. 'My afternoon meeting is going to drag intolerably.'

He had missed her, Ramon acknowledged. The thought caused his dark brows to draw together. No woman had ever been important enough in his life for him to miss being with her, and he was startled to realise just how often he had thought about Lauren while he had been away. But he did not intend to share that information with her. He did not want her to think she could ever be more to him than his mistress.

His frown deepened as his thoughts turned once more to the news that his father's cancer had returned after a brief period of remission. This time it was incurable. Now he understood why lately the Duque had been more insistent than ever that he should choose a suitable bride—with emphasis on the word *suitable*, Ramon thought grimly, recalling how his father had raked up the old story of Catalina during their last conversation.

Catalina Cortez was a mistake from his past of whom he did not like to be reminded, he brooded irritably. *Dios*, he had been a testosterone-fuelled eighteen-year-old when he had lost his heart and his head to the gorgeous glamour model whose bountiful curves had been regularly displayed on the pages of certain top-shelf magazines. But almost two decades later his father still would not allow him to forget that he had been utterly determined to marry Catalina.

Ramon did not suppose he was the first man to have been made a fool of by love, but he had learned his lesson well and he would not be a fool again. The memory of discovering Catalina with her lover and realising that she was a slut who had only been so flatteringly eager to marry him to get her greedy hands on the Velaquez fortune still touched a raw nerve—but no more than the humiliation he had felt that his father had been proved right.

Far worse than Catalina's treachery had been the knowledge that he had disappointed his family. But it had been a long time ago, Ramon thought impatiently. Since then he had assured his father that he was prepared to do his duty by marrying a woman suitable to be a *duquesa* and to beget an heir. Now it seemed that assurances were no longer enough. His father was dying and wanted to see his only son married. Duty was calling him in an ever louder voice, and the freedom to take his pleasure with mistresses was drawing to an end—for when he did marry he intended to be a faithful husband to his as yet unknown bride.

'Ramon, are you still there?' Lauren's voice dragged him from his thoughts. 'It must be a bad signal. I thought I'd lost you for a moment.'

'I am still here,' Ramon replied smoothly. 'I'll see you tonight.' He ended the call and stared out at the London traffic, conscious that his earlier feeling of contentment had evaporated.

Lauren arrived at the restaurant ten minutes early, and went to the bar to wait. Butterflies were leaping in her stomach at the prospect of seeing Ramon again. She had missed him badly while he had been away, and wondering how he would react to the life-changing news she was about to tell him exacerbated her tension.

Even though her back was to the door she knew the exact moment he walked into the restaurant by the startled silence that fell, followed by a ripple of curiosity in the voices of the diners and those, like her, at the bar. She turned her head and her knees felt weak.

Six foot four, with heart-stopping good-looks and a simmering sensual magnetism, he drew interested glances wherever he went. Mainly from women, Lauren thought ruefully as she noticed an attractive brunette who was sitting at the bar attempt to gain his attention by crossing her legs so that her skirt rode up her thigh.

But who could blame the woman? Ramon was utterly gorgeous, she thought helplessly, her heart-rate quickening when he strode towards her. His dark eyes focused on her face, seemingly oblivious to every other female in the room. His superbly tailored suit drew attention to his broad shoulders and lean, hard body, while the bright lights of the restaurant danced over his bronzed, chiselled features and made his black hair gleam like raw silk. As he came nearer his sensual mouth curved into a smile that touched her soul—a smile that was just for her and made her feel as if she was special to him.

She hadn't planned to fall in love with him. Until Ramon had swept into her life she had been scornful of love, and although she had had other relationships they had been conducted on her terms and had left her emotions untouched. But Ramon was different. From the very beginning she had felt at ease with him; he was witty and intelligent, with a wicked sense of humour, and she enjoyed his company.

The fact that he was an incredible lover who had given her the confidence to explore her intensely passionate nature was just one reason why he had captured her heart—although at this moment it was a very pressing reason, she acknowledged, conscious that her nipples had hardened and now felt acutely sensitive as they rubbed against the silk bustier she was wearing beneath her jacket.

He was so close now that she could inhale the familiar spicy scent of his cologne, and the urge to fling her arms around his neck and press her lips feverishly over his face, his mouth, was almost irresistible. But she did resist, knowing that he would be appalled by such a public display. Ramon guarded his privacy fiercely, and only ever kissed her when they were alone. But when he halted in front of her and she saw the genuine warmth in his smile she gave up trying to act cool and beamed at him.

'You look gorgeous, *querida*,' Ramon greeted her, heat flaring inside him as he raked his eyes over Lauren's tight-fitting, pillar-box-red skirt, and settled on the tantalising confection of silk and lace visible beneath her jacket. 'And very sexy. I'm amazed the male lawyers at your firm can concentrate on their work when you are such a delicious distraction.'

'I wore a high-necked, very prim blouse to the office,' Lauren assured him. 'But I thought you would appreciate it if I changed into something more decorative.' The low-cut black silk bustier which revealed a daring amount of cleavage had cost a fortune, but the flare of dull colour that winged along Ramon's cheekbones told her it was worth every penny.

'I will demonstrate my appreciation all night long,' he promised her huskily.

The heat inside him was now a burning throb of need that was centred in his groin and caused his blood to pound through his veins. Lauren was a delectable package of honey-blonde hair and vo-luptuous curves, and it was not surprising he had missed her, Ramon assured himself. He was sorely tempted to pull her into his arms and plunder her pouting scarlet lips in a searing kiss until she clung to him, trembling and eager, but with an enormous effort of will he controlled himself.

It was not only the Spanish paparazzi who were fascinated by the son of one of the nation's most prominent and wealthy families. The English media had labelled him the most eligible bachelor in Europe, and a picture of him kissing a blonde in a bar would make the kind of headlines he was determined to avoid. And so, nostrils flaring as he breathed in the floral fragrance of Lauren's perfume, he placed his hand lightly on her waist and propelled her out of the bar.

'I believe our table is ready.' He dipped his head towards her as they followed a waiter, and murmured, 'Let's hope service is quick tonight, *querida*, because I am *very* hungry.'

The gleam in his eyes left Lauren in no doubt of his meaning, and a quiver of excitement ran the length of her spine. After two weeks apart she ached for him to make love to her. Soon they would go back to his apartment. But first—her heart skittered—first she must tell him that she was expecting his baby.

She simply did not know how he was going to react to her accidental pregnancy. For unquestionably it *was* an accident—caused by one forgetful moment when they had shared a shower, she remembered ruefully. She had not planned to have a baby at this stage of her life, and had spent the past week veering between panic and disbelief. But, strangely, the moment she had seen Ramon tonight the baby had become real to her—no longer simply a blue line on the pregnancy test, but a new life growing inside her, created by her and the man she loved.

She caught her bottom lip with her teeth. Would

Ramon feel the same way? He had never made any reference to the future, and although he was a wonderful lover who treated her with consideration and respect she did not know how he really felt about her. But he *had* invited her to dinner tonight to celebrate their six-month anniversary, Lauren reminded herself. Surely that meant something?

The waiter took their drinks order. Ramon made no comment when she requested fruit juice, because she had told him when they had first met that she disliked alcohol—although not her reasons for being strictly teetotal. The memory of how her mother had regularly drowned her sorrows in gin after her father had left them was something Lauren never spoke about to anyone.

With impressive speed the waiter returned with their drinks, and Ramon lifted his glass of champagne. 'I'd like to make a toast—to another successful take-over bid by Velaquez Conglomerates.'

Lauren froze—until the lengthening silence became awkward, and then she hurriedly snatched up her glass of juice. 'Oh…yes—to Velaquez Conglomerates.' She touched her glass to Ramon's and gave him a tentative smile, which faltered when he made no mention of the other reason they were celebrating.

'So, tell me what you've been doing while I was away,' Ramon said comfortably.

It was not a question he had been prone to asking his previous lovers, he mused. Usually he was bored to death by the details of shopping and celebrity gossip that most women seemed to find so fascinating, but Lauren was a highly intelligent corporate lawyer, and he enjoyed discussing their respective careers, or the latest political thriller by an author they both admired.

Lauren could recall little of the past two weeks other than the mind-numbing panic that had swamped her after she had discovered she was pregnant. She could think of nothing to say, and instead fumbled in her handbag and handed Ramon a small gift-wrapped package.

'It's a present,' she told him when he viewed the package suspiciously, as if he expected it to blow up in his face. 'It's nothing, really.' She could feel hot colour flooding her cheeks. 'Just a little token…to celebrate our anniversary.'

Ramon stiffened, and the sense of impending disaster he had felt when he had spoken to Lauren earlier in the day settled over him like a black cloud. 'Anniversary?' he queried coolly.

'It's six months since we met. I thought that was what we were celebrating—the reason you'd arranged for us to have dinner at the restaurant where you brought me on our first date…' Lauren's voice trailed away. She stared at Ramon's shocked expression and cringed with embarrassment as it became apparent that she had got things very wrong. 'I thought you had remembered,' she muttered, wishing that a hole would open in the floor beneath her chair and swallow her up.

Ramon regarded her in a taut silence. 'I must admit I did not,' he said bluntly, frowning as the implication of her words sank in. Six months! How had so much time passed without him noticing it? And how had Lauren insinuated herself into his life so subtly that he had grown used to her being there? Ordinarily he never dated women for more than a few weeks before he reached his boredom threshold. But even though she had been his mistress for half a year Lauren never bored him— either in bed or out—he acknowledged grimly. He hadn't even been tempted to look at another woman.

His frown deepened. *Dios!* He had been faithful to her without realising the longevity of their affair, but now that she had made him aware of it he was shocked that he had allowed what had started off as just another casual fling to continue for so long. He felt as though it was Lauren's fault. If she had started to irritate him—or, as so often happened with his mistresses, shown possessive tendencies—he would have ended the affair months ago. But she had been the perfect mistress: undemanding, and happy to take a discreet role in his life. Her desire to celebrate an anniversary was like a bolt from the blue. It had overstepped a line in their relationship, Ramon brooded, annoyance replacing his contentment of a few minutes ago.

'I do not set great store by anniversaries,' he told her curtly.

Impeccable manners forced him to untie the gold ribbon on top of the package, and he parted the wrapping paper to reveal a striped silk tie in muted shades of blue and grey. It was exactly the sort of thing he would have chosen for himself, but the realisation that Lauren knew his tastes so well did not improve his temper.

He looked up to find her watching him anxiously, and it struck him that she had seemed unusually tense since he had greeted her at the bar.

'It's charming,' he said, forcing a smile as he lifted the tie from its wrapping. 'An excellent choice. *Gracias.*'

'I told you it was only a small gift,' she mumbled, sounding defensive.

But it was not the size or the value of the present that was a problem. It was the reason *why* she had given it to him that disturbed him, Ramon mused. Lauren had never seemed the type who indulged in sentimental gestures, and it was disconcerting to think that he might not know her quite as well as he had believed.

Thankfully the waiter arrived with their first course, and while they ate he steered the conversation away from the contentious topic of their so-called anniversary to a discussion about the mixed reviews for a new play that had opened in the West End.

The food at the Vine was always superb, but afterwards Lauren had no recollection of what she had eaten. She ordered a camomile tea to end the meal, and sipped it frantically to try and counteract her queasiness induced by the aroma of Ramon's coffee. Usually she loved coffee, but for the past week just the smell of it had been enough to send her running to the bathroom.

Morning sickness—which seemed to strike at any time during the day—was a physical indication that her pregnancy was real, and if she was honest she felt scared and uncertain of the future. *Tell Ramon about the baby now*, her brain insisted. But she could not forget his harsh tone when he had announced that he did not set much store by anniversaries, and the words *I'm pregnant* remained trapped in her throat.

Ramon's reaction to her innocuous gift had been

bad enough. He had made her feel like a criminal for wanting to celebrate the fact that their relationship was special to her. Clearly it was not special to him, she thought miserably. But the stark fact remained that she was expecting his baby, and sooner or later he was going to have to know.

During dinner she'd managed to smile and chat to him as if her humiliating discovery that their anniversary meant nothing to him had never happened. Ramon certainly seemed to have put it out of his mind. But when he draped his arm around her shoulders in the back of his limousine and instructed the chauffeur to take them to his apartment overlooking Hyde Park, anger slowly replaced the hurt inside her. If they did not have a relationship that was worth celebrating, what *did* they have? she wondered bitterly.

The car purred into the underground car park beneath his apartment block. Moments later they entered the lift and he pulled her into his arms.

'Alone, finally,' Ramon murmured in a satisfied voice. Lauren's perfume tantalised his senses, and his breathing quickened when he took the clip from her chignon and ran his fingers though the mass of silky blonde hair that tumbled to her shoulders. *Dios*, he was hungry for her. She was like a fever in his blood. With a muttered oath he covered her mouth with his and teased her lips apart with his tongue to plunder her moist warmth.

The unsettled feeling that had dogged him throughout dinner faded when he felt her instant response. For a few moments he had wondered if he was going to have to end their affair, and he was surprised by his reluctance to do so.

But once a mistress started to mention anniversaries it was time she became an ex-mistress—because how could you celebrate what was essentially a casual sexual relationship? He had thought Lauren understood the rules, and he was relieved that it seemed now, after all, that she did. She had made no further reference to the amount of time they had been together, and when she pressed her soft, curvaceous body against him his doubts were swept away by the thunderous intensity of his desire.

He steered her out of the lift and through the front door of his apartment without lifting his lips from hers. His hands deftly tugged off her jacket and set to work unlacing the front of the sexy bustier while he backed her along the hall towards his bedroom.

How could she resist him? Lauren thought despairingly, her body trembling with anticipation. Soon he would be caressing her naked flesh. With his dark hair falling over his brow, his jacket and tie flung carelessly to the floor and his shirt now open to the waist, to reveal a muscular, bronzed chest covered with a mass of wiry dark hairs, he was lethally sexy—but, more than that, he was her world.

But she wasn't *his*. The thought forced its way into her head, and her mouth quivered beneath the demanding pressure of his kiss. Her legs hit the end of the bed at the same time as he loosened the bustier and her breasts spilled into his hands.

'I missed you, *querida*,' Ramon groaned hoarsely.

But instead of his words soothing her battered pride they caused her to stiffen and draw back from him.

'Did you miss *me*—or sex with me?' she asked him tremulously, watching him with wary grey eyes when he frowned.

'Don't play games,' he said impatiently. 'It's one and the same thing. Of course I missed having sex with you. After all, you *are* my mistress.'

The blood drained from Lauren's face, and she could have sworn she actually heard the ripping sound of her heart being slashed by sharp knives as her pathetic hopes crumbled to dust.

'I am *not* your mistress,' she said tightly, gritting her teeth to stop herself from wailing like a distraught child—because that was how she felt.

Just as she had as a little girl, when she had witnessed her pony bolt out of the field into the path of a lorry, or as a teenager when she had watched her adored father walk down the garden path and out of her life for ever.

She stepped away from Ramon and clutched the edges of the bustier together, her hands shaking. 'A mistress is a kept woman, and you do *not* keep me. I have my own flat, a job, and I pay my own way.'

'You virtually live at my apartment when I am in London,' Ramon reminded her tersely. He was frustrated that Lauren was wasting time arguing when all he could think about was thrusting his throbbing erection between her soft thighs.

'True. But I keep the fridge stocked with your favourite foods—including caviar and champagne—and I take your suits to the cleaners. They are only little things, I know, but I try to balance out our living costs fairly.'

Irritated beyond measure, Ramon raked a hand through his hair. How on earth had he allowed his affair with Lauren to evolve into such cosy domesticity that she dealt with his dry-cleaning? That was the sort of thing a wife did, not a mistress. And how were they even having this conversation when seconds ago they had been on the verge of making love?

Having sex, he corrected himself. Love was certainly not a factor of their relationship. Yes, she had become important to him, he admitted. More so than he had realised until he'd spent the past couple of weeks missing her like hell. But, whether she agreed or not, she *was* his mistress. The course of his life had been determined from birth, and the responsibilities that came with being a member of the Spanish nobility meant that she could never be anything else.

Tension thrummed between them, and the un-edifying label of *mistress* drummed in Lauren's brain. She had thought they were lovers who shared an equal relationship, but clearly Ramon did not view her in that way. Her voice sounded rusty when she forced herself to speak. 'I…need to know where we're going,' she said baldly.

Dark eyebrows winged upwards in an expression of arrogant amusement, and sherry-brown eyes rested insolently on the unlaced bustier that she was clutching across her breasts. 'I had thought we were going to bed,' Ramon drawled.

The flare of hurt in her eyes tugged on his conscience, and he cursed his quick temper. But, *Dios mio*, she had started this ridiculous conversation. He was tempted to snatch her back into his arms and kiss her until she melted into submission, but she looked as fragile as spun glass tonight—something he had only just noticed, he thought grimly. He wondered if she was ill. She was certainly upset. But why was she insisting on defining the nature of their affair when it worked perfectly well for both of them without the need for explanation?

'I mean where our relationship is going,' Lauren said with quiet dignity.

Sick fear churned in her stomach. Under ordinary circumstances Ramon's forbidding expression would have warned her not to proceed with a conversation that felt horribly as if it was going to smash full-pelt into a brick wall. But these were not ordinary circumstances. She was pregnant with his child, and her instinct to do the best for her baby was more important than her pride.

'Tell me honestly: do you envisage us having any kind of future together?' she asked quietly. 'Or am I just another blonde to temporarily share your bed?'

His silence confirmed what her heart already knew.

Ramon's eyes narrowed. 'I have never made false promises, or led you to believe that I wanted more than an affair. You never hid the fact that your career plays a major part in your life, and I thought you were content with a relationship that did not put the pressure of unrealistic expectations on either of us.'

She had never had expectations, Lauren thought sadly. But she had hoped that she was beginning to mean something to him. How could she have been such a fool? she asked herself angrily. She had been blinded by her love for Ramon, and had kidded herself that the companionship they shared was proof that he cared for her. Now she knew that he had only ever regarded her as a convenient mistress—who provided sex and entertaining conversation on demand, but never made demands of her own.

As for her career… Her hand moved instinctively to her stomach. She had worked hard to become a lawyer, and undoubtedly her job was important to her. But in eight months time she was going to take on the most important role a woman could fulfil—and it looked increasingly as though she was going to be bringing up her baby on her own.

She stared at Ramon's perfectly sculpted features and her heart clenched. 'Things change,' she said huskily. 'Life can't stay the same or we would stagnate. How do you see *your* future, Ramon? I mean…' her voice shook slightly '…do you ever want to marry?'

This was not how he had envisaged spending his first night back in London, Ramon thought furiously. Up until now he had been clinging to the hope that this new Lauren, who had broken the unwritten rules of their liaison by demanding to discuss it, would suddenly metamorphose back into the familiar, delightfully easygoing Lauren, whose sole aim had always seemed to be to please him in bed. He was outraged that she had brought up the thorny subject of marriage, but now that she had asked he did not intend to lie to her.

'The Velaquez family are among the oldest members of the Spanish nobility, and can trace their ancestors back to the eleventh century,' he told her harshly. 'As the only son of the Duque de Velaquez it is my duty to marry a bride from another aristocratic Spanish family and provide an heir to continue the bloodline of Velaquez.'

'You're the son of a *duke*?' Lauren said faintly, stunned by the revelation. She had thought that the supreme self-confidence which sometimes revealed itself as arrogance was simply his nature. But he was a titled member of the Spanish nobility—it was small wonder he had a regal air about him.

'The title will pass to me on the death of my father,' Ramon said tersely, feeling a shaft of pain when he thought of his father's prognosis. The Duque had always been a strict, rather remote parent, and Ramon's childhood had been dominated by rules and stifling formality, but sadly lacking in displays of affection. He had always respected his father, but it was only now that he realised he also loved him, and it was for that reason more than any other that he intended to one day fulfil his duty and marry a woman suitable to fill the role of Duquesa.

He stared grimly at Lauren, and was infuriated by the hurt he could see in her grey eyes. *Dios*, he had never given her any reason to believe that their affair might lead to him offering her a permanent place in his life. They had a good routine that suited both of them, and he wished they could abandon this discussion that had no purpose and lose themselves in the fiery passion that had blazed between them from the moment they had first met.

He took a deep breath. Perhaps, if he was patient, he could salvage the evening. Now that he had explained his situation to Lauren he could see no reason why their affair should not continue. Duty beckoned him, but, his father's illness aside, he was in no hurry to sacrifice his freedom and choose a bride.

'What is the point in worrying about the future when the present is so enjoyable?' he murmured, stepping closer to her and lifting his hand to stroke her hair back from her face. She instantly shrank away from him, and his jaw hardened.

How could she do anything else *but* worry about the future? Lauren thought wildly. 'Let me get this straight. You intend to marry—not necessarily for love—you will choose a bride who is of suitably noble birth in order to have a child—presumably it will have to be a boy—who will carry on your family name,' she said slowly.

Ramon's mouth tightened at her insistence on carrying on with the conversation when he had made it clear that he wanted to drop it. 'As I have explained, it is my duty to ensure the continuation of the Velaquez line,' he said curtly. 'When my father dies I will return to Spain to live at the historic family home, the Castillo del Toro, and it is important that I have a son who will one day take my place.'

'You live in a castle!' Maybe this was all part of some horrible nightmare, Lauren thought desperately, and soon she would wake up and find that Ramon had *not* turned into an icy stranger who inhabited the rarefied world of the Spanish nobility which an ordinary English lawyer from Swindon could never belong to.

Duty was such a cold word, she thought with a shiver. Ramon did not sound as though he planned to have a child because he wanted to be a father, but because it was necessary for him to produce an heir. But would he want the baby she was carrying? Would he demand that she marry him so that his half-English child would be his legal heir? Or—and this seemed more likely—would he offer her money? Maybe buy somewhere for her and the baby to live and pay his illegitimate child the occasional duty visit, retaining his freedom to marry a woman suitable to be his *duquesa*, who could give him a child with noble Spanish blood running through its veins?

A primitive maternal instinct to protect her child swept through Lauren. She stared at Ramon and saw him for what he really was—a ruthless billionaire businessman. It struck her then that she had never known him at all. He had acted the role of charming lover, but he had never allowed her to see the real man, the son of a *duque*, whose home was a castle. And in that moment she decided that she must keep her baby a secret from him. Ramon needed an heir to continue the Velaquez name, but her baby deserved a father who would love it unconditionally. It would be better for her child to have no father at all than one who did not love it, and would perhaps make him or her feel inadequate and not worthy of the Velaquez name.

Never the most patient of men, Ramon had suddenly had enough of being grilled by Lauren. 'Is there any point to this conversation?' he demanded explosively.

She hesitated, sure that the painful thudding of her heart could not be good for the baby. 'I think there is,' she said sombrely. 'I felt it was time to establish what kind of relationship we have, and it's clear that we view things very differently. I am *not* your mistress,' she insisted fiercely, when he lifted his brows sardonically.

His eyes dropped deliberately to the sexy silk bustier that barely covered her breasts. 'Yet, like a good mistress, you dressed to please me,' he drawled, his mouth curving into a hard smile when she blushed scarlet and frantically pulled the laces together. 'A mistress is all you can ever be to me, *querida*.' He could not pretend that there were any other possibilities.

The careless endearment tore at her heart, but she refused to cry in front of him. The tears could come later, when she was alone—which was likely to be for a very long time, she thought dismally.

'In that case I would like to go home,' she whispered. 'And…and I won't be coming back.'

Incredulity ripped through Ramon, but his disbelief that Lauren appeared to be dumping him swiftly turned to outrage. Although he had ended more affairs than he cared to remember, no woman had ever broken up with *him* before.

'*Dios!* What do you expect from me?' he demanded furiously. 'Would you rather I made false promises I can never keep?' He did not want to lose her, but he was certainly not going to plead with her to change her mind. It was not as if he needed her. There were plenty more attractive blondes willing to share his bed.

He regarded her arrogantly, the noble lines of his illustrious ancestry etched onto his perfectly sculpted features. 'If you really want to leave then I will arrange for my driver to take you home,' he informed her in an icy tone. 'But once you walk out of the door our arrangement is over, and I will not have you back.'

Lauren felt numb beyond words as it hit her that this really was the end. 'I just want to go,' she said huskily. She stiffened when he caught her chin and forced her face up to meet his angry gaze. Tension throbbed between them. For a moment she thought he was going to kiss her, and she despaired that she would have the strength to resist him, but then he swore savagely and flung her from him.

'Go, then,' he said savagely. And without another word she fled.

CHAPTER ONE

EIGHTEEN months later, Lauren hurried through the open-plan office of the big City law firm where she worked, and gave a silent groan when she checked the time on her watch. The staccato tap of her stiletto heels on the tiled floor came to an abrupt halt when Guy Hadlow stepped in front of her.

'The old man has been asking for you since nine o'clock this morning. He wants to see you in his office as soon as you arrive.' Guy gave her a malicious grin. 'You're forty-five minutes late. Did you fancy a lie-in? You look like you had a heavy night.'

'Not that my being late is any of your business, but it's snowing in the North London suburbs and my train was cancelled,' Lauren told him tersely.

Like her, Guy was a lawyer at Plessy, Gambrill and Hess, working in the commercial property department. The only son of a wealthy banker, he was used to having what he wanted. Lauren's polite but consistent refusal to date him had revealed an unpleasant side to his nature. The fact that they were now in competition for the same promotion had exacerbated the hostility between them.

As for her having a lie-in! That would be the day, she thought ruefully. Her ten-month-old son, Mateo, was cutting another tooth, and Lauren couldn't remember the last time she'd had a full night's sleep. Matty had woken at five that morning, and after she had given him his early-morning bottle and changed his nappy she had showered, dressed, loaded the washing machine and unloaded the dishwasher before bundling him into his all-in-one suit and into the car.

The icy roads had caused the traffic to crawl, the usual ten-minute drive to the daycare nursery had taken double that, and when she had finally arrived she'd had no time to do more than thrust Mateo into the arms of one of the staff before dashing off to the station. The sound of his pitiful sobs had haunted her throughout her journey to work, and she was in no mood to put up with Guy's sarcastic wit.

'Do you know why Mr Gambrill wants to see me?'

Guy shrugged. 'I'm just the messenger boy. But

it's a pity you chose this morning to turn up late. That won't help your chances of promotion.'

'I didn't *choose* to be late,' Lauren snapped, feeling her stomach swoop down towards her toes. Alistair Gambrill headed the commercial property department at PGH—a senior partner who did not suffer fools gladly and was a stickler for punctuality. But if he had asked to see her at nine o'clock he could not have known then that she had been delayed, so it was unlikely that he wanted to discuss her time-keeping, Lauren reasoned.

Brow furrowed in a frown as she silently debated the reason for the summons, she dumped her coat and handbag on her desk and hurried along the corridor towards her boss's office suite. His PA was speaking on the phone, and while she waited she made a lightning study of her appearance in the mirror behind the secretary's desk.

Her pillar-box-red suit was stylish and defiantly bright on yet another grey February day. Her crisp white blouse added a touch of professionalism, and thankfully there was no sign of the blob of baby sick on her shoulder, which she had scrubbed off on her way out of her flat that morning. But Guy was right. The dark circles beneath her eyes which could not be completely concealed with foundation *were* an indication of regular sleepless nights.

The joys of being a single mother, she thought

heavily. Yet, given the choice, she would not change things. Her son had been unexpected and unplanned, but she loved him with a fierce intensity that was beyond anything she had ever experienced. Just thinking about Matty's darling little face, his shock of black hair and enormous sherry-brown eyes made her heart clench.

The PA put down the phone and gave Lauren a brief smile. 'Go straight in. Mr Gambrill is waiting for you.'

Had there been a tiny emphasis on the word *waiting*? As she opened the door Lauren made a frantic mental check-list of recently completed assignments, as well as the current commercial property transactions she was working on. Had she made a mistake that she was unaware of? Had a client filed a complaint about her work? The purchase of a new office block for a well-known City bank was taking longer than expected after problems had arisen with the wording of the lease.

'Ah, Lauren.'

To her surprise Alistair Gambrill sounded delighted to see her, rather than annoyed at her lateness. But she barely heard him. As she entered the office her eyes were riveted on the second man in the room, who rose to his feet and subjected her to an arrogant scrutiny that made her blood run cold.

Her steps faltered. Every muscle in her body clenched in fierce rejection and she could feel the blood drain from her face. This could not be happening, she thought dazedly. Ramon could not be here, strolling towards her with the easy grace she remembered so well.

Alistair's attention was focused on his guest, so he was oblivious to the fact that his member of staff had whitened to the colour of the pristine blotting pad on his desk. 'Lauren, I'd like you to meet our new client, Ramon Velaquez. Ramon, may I introduce one of PGH's finest commercial property lawyers, Lauren Maitland?'

One of the company's finest lawyers! That was news to her, Lauren thought blankly. But Alistair was smiling at her as if she was his favourite niece. He was clearly keen to impress Ramon, and she sensed his impatience as he waited for her to speak.

She could feel her heart slamming against her ribs. Should she reveal to Alistair that she was already acquainted with the client? She choked back a hysterical laugh. *Acquainted* seemed such an old-fashioned word, but what else could she say—that she and Ramon had once been lovers? Would *he* explain that they knew each other?

Somehow she forced her throat to work. 'Mr Velaquez.'

'Ramon, please. Let us dispense with formality.'

His voice was just as Lauren remembered it: deep, melodious, with a faint huskiness that was spine-tinglingly sexy. It tugged on her soul like a siren's song, drawing her gaze inexorably to his face.

Matty had his father's eyes, she thought faintly. The likeness between them was almost uncanny. When her son had been born and the midwife had placed him in her arms she had stared in awe at his tiny face and been reminded of Ramon. But her joy had been tinged with an aching sadness that he was not with her to welcome their child into the world. She had never expected to see him again, but now, unbelievably, he was here in Alistair Gambrill's office, and she was overwhelmed by the conflicting emotions that stormed through her.

'I'm pleased to meet you, Lauren.' Only Ramon could make her name sound so sensual, his discernible accent lingering over the vowels like a lover's caress, causing the tiny hairs on her arms to stand on end.

Her face suddenly felt hot as the blood moved in her veins once more. Even worse was the instant effect Ramon had on her body, and she bit back a gasp when she felt her nipples tighten so that they strained uncomfortably against the lacy restriction of her bra.

Why was he here? she wondered fearfully, tension knotting in her stomach. Could he have found out about Mateo? She glanced desperately at Alistair. Everyone at PGH knew she had a son. Had her boss unwittingly revealed her secret by explaining to Ramon that her lateness this morning might have been due to childcare issues?

She fought the frantic urge to turn and flee from Ramon's speculative gaze. Alistair had introduced him as a new client, she reminded herself. He *couldn't* be here because of Matty. But he had known the name of the law firm she had moved to shortly before they had broken up, and she was sure his presence at PGH was not merely coincidence. Nothing Ramon ever did was unplanned.

What game was he playing? she wondered. But it was easier to go along with it in front of Alistair than to admit to a history that was well and truly in the past. Pride and professionalism were her only weapons against Ramon's lethal charm, and she called on both, forcing her lips to curve into a polite smile as she extended her hand. 'And I am delighted to meet you…' She paused infinitesimally while she steeled herself to say his name. 'Ramon.'

In the few brief seconds before his hand closed around hers she allowed her gaze to roam over him. It was only eighteen months since she had last seen him, but he looked older. Still stunningly handsome, but there were a few faint lines around his eyes, and his aristocratic features seemed harder somehow, his skin drawn tight over his slashing cheekbones. The silky black hair that had once touched his collar was now cropped short— less jet-setting playboy, more billionaire business- man, she mused.

She had read in the newspapers of his fa- ther's death a year ago. Ramon was now CEO of Velaquez Conglomerates, which included among its business interests the famous Velaquez winery, a bank, and a chain of five-star hotels around the world. He must also have assumed the title of Duque de Velaquez, she realised. But then her thoughts scattered as his hand clasped hers, his strong, tanned fingers contrasting starkly with her paler skin, and the contact of flesh on flesh sent an electrical current shooting up her arm and a quiver of reaction down her spine.

Ramon studied Lauren in a leisurely appraisal, frowning slightly as he felt his body's involun- tary response to her. His arousal was instant and embarrassingly hard. He was not a testosterone- fuelled youth, he reminded himself, irritated to discover that his desire for her had not lessened in the year and a half since he had last seen her.

She was wearing the scarlet suit she had worn

the night she had abruptly ended their relationship—although today she had teamed it with a demure white blouse rather than the black silk bustier that had displayed her breasts like plump velvety peaches. Her close-fitting jacket showed off her slim waist, while her pencil-skirt moulded her hips and stopped several inches above her knees to reveal long slender legs in sheer hose. Black patent stiletto heels added another three inches to her height and made her legs seem even longer—he wondered if she still liked to wear stockings.

He inhaled swiftly, and tore his eyes and his over-active imagination away from her legs. Her face was attractive, rather than pretty, oval in shape, with creamy skin, intelligent grey eyes beneath hazel brows. Her dark honey-blonde was hair swept up into a chignon.

What was it about this woman that he found such a turn-on? Ramon wondered irritably. He had dated some of the world's most beautiful women—actresses and models whose looks were their fortune. Only this graceful English rose had taken him to the edge of sexual insanity.

The passion they had shared had been mind-blowing—the best he'd ever known. Although he had refused to admit the intensity of his need for her during their affair. The last eighteen months had passed swiftly—his father's illness and subsequent death had been followed by a period of mourning, while at the same time he had taken his place at the head of the company, endeavouring to please shareholders and trying to comfort his mother and sisters. There had been little time for introspection, yet memories of Lauren—the silky softness of her hair, her taut, slender body, the soft cries she let out when he made love to her—had continued to invade his mind.

She had become a thorn in his flesh, he acknowledged grimly. A persistent ache that he had put down to sexual frustration but which, for some reason, he had been unable to assuage with other women. Now he was back in London to oversee a business project—but it was also an ideal opportunity to discover if his lingering sexual attraction to his ex-mistress was real, or a memory that he should have dismissed from his mind months ago.

'Please have a seat, Ramon. I know you have a tight schedule, and we have plenty to discuss.' Alistair Gambrill's voice sliced through the aching silence, although the man seemed unaware of the tension in the room.

Lauren tried to pull her hand free from Ramon's grasp, but he retained his hold for few more seconds, his eyes narrowing on her flushed face before he finally released her.

He already had his answer, Ramon brooded. His desire for Lauren was not imagined. In fact his imagination was enjoying a highly erotic fantasy in which they were alone in the office and she was spread across the desk, with her skirt rucked up around her waist and her long, shapely legs wrapped around him.

Eighteen months ago he had been furious when she had walked out on him, and had vowed to dismiss her from his mind. But he had been unable to forget her. There was still unfinished business between them. The flare of emotion in her eyes when she had first entered Alistair Gambrill's office, and the slight tremble of her hand when she had placed it in his were evidence that she was not as immune to him as her cool smile would have him believe.

Lauren's legs were trembling as the shock of Ramon's unexpected appearance seeped through her, and she sank weakly onto the chair next to him. She had no idea why Alistair had summoned her to meet this new client, but while she was trying to guess the reason the senior lawyer cleared his throat.

'I have studied your remit, Ramon, and it all seems straightforward. As I understand it, Velaquez Conglomerates are looking to purchase a number of suitable commercial properties in

London, with the intention of applying for planning permission to run these establishments as wine bars.'

Ramon nodded. 'That's correct. I would like to open two, maybe three bars here in the capital. I already have a shortlist of potential properties suggested by estate agents, and what I require is a commercial property lawyer who will work exclusively on this project and who has additional expertise in planning and development laws.'

He turned his head and looked directly at Lauren, his predatory smile reminding her of a wolf stalking its prey. 'Put simply, I need *you*, Lauren. I understand that you have specialised particularly in Town and Country planning matters, and I believe you are best suited to advise me on any potential problems with the properties I am interested in.'

She gaped at him, her mind reeling in horror as it sank in that he seemed to be suggesting that he wanted her to work for him. 'There are several other commercial property lawyers at PGH who are more qualified and experienced than I am— and who I am sure would suit your requirements b-better,' she stammered quickly, glancing frantically at Alistair for confirmation.

Ramon's eyes narrowed on her flushed face. 'I have read the reports on your recent assignments and I am impressed by your work,' he said coolly. 'I also noted on your CV that you studied Spanish and speak it fluently, which would be additionally useful,' he added, the gleam in his eyes telling her that he had been aware before he had read her CV that she could speak his language.

He turned back to Alistair Gambrill before she could comment. 'I understand that PGH promote a service whereby Lauren could be seconded to Velaquez Conglomerates to give personalised in-house legal advice until the project is completed?'

Alistair nodded enthusiastically. 'That is certainly possible. The in-house legal practice offered by our company is fairly unique, and enables companies such as your own to access specialist lawyers without having to employ their own full-time solicitor.'

'So in effect Lauren would be working directly for Velaquez Conglomerates until the project is finalised?' Ramon queried. 'Can I take it you would be happy with that, Lauren?'

This time there was no mistaking the predatory nature of his smile; the hard gleam in his eyes told her that he could read her mind.

Apprehension churned in the pit of her stomach. *No*, she damned well would *not* be happy, she wanted to cry. How could she work for him, spend hours every day with him, and manage to keep Matty a secret from him? Once again she felt a desperate urge to flee, to run out of the office and keep on running. But if she did that she was highly likely to lose her job, her only means of supporting her son, and so she remained in her chair and knotted her trembling fingers together as Alistair spoke.

'I have no doubt that you will find Lauren a dedicated and hard-working employee who will do her utmost to please you.'

'That's good to hear.' The wolfish smile widened, and despite her tension the wicked glint in Ramon's eyes sent heat coursing through Lauren's veins.

Utterly dismayed by her reaction to him, she did not trust herself to speak. But inside she felt sick with panic. She would have to speak to Alistair privately later, she decided frantically. But what excuse could she give for not wanting to work for an influential new client? For now at least she would have to go along with it.

'I will certainly do my best to ensure that all transactions are completed as smoothly and quickly as possible,' she said coolly.

'Good.' Ramon smiled, showing his white teeth, and Lauren felt a sharp pain, as if she had been kicked in the ribs. Missing him had become a part of her life, a persistent ache in her chest, and she quickly compressed her lips to disguise their betraying quiver.

'I hope to open at least one wine bar this summer,' he continued, his eyes fixed intently on her, 'which is why I want you to give your exclusive attention to this project. We will need to liaise on a daily basis, and an office will be made available for you at my London headquarters.'

'Oh, but...' This time she refused to keep silent, despite Alistair's warning frown. 'I think it would be better if I remained here at PGH. I'm responsible for several other accounts—'

'I will personally allocate other members of staff to take over those accounts,' Alistair interrupted smoothly.

Lauren guessed he was very eager for her to work directly for Ramon. The in-house legal practice might save clients the expense of employing their own full-time corporate lawyer, but PGH charged high fees for the service.

'I'll have a contract drawn up immediately, and Lauren is at your disposal as of now.'

'Excellent.'

The satisfaction in Ramon's voice sparked Lauren's temper. She did not want to work for Velaquez Conglomerates, and she certainly did not want to work for Ramon. But to object would be tantamount to suicide for her career. This was a fantastic opportunity for her to prove her suitability for the upcoming promotion at PGH, and a higher position would mean a rise in her salary, which would help with Matty's exorbitant nursery fees. But she couldn't shake off the idea that Ramon had deliberately engineered the situation. The million dollar question was *why*? What did he want from her?

She was agonisingly aware of him sitting beside her. The spicy tang of his cologne assailed her senses, so achingly familiar that she felt a sudden constriction in her throat. Her eyes were drawn to his face, searching for an answer that was not forthcoming, and instead she glimpsed a ruthless determination in his gaze that sent a prickle of unease down her spine. The moment passed, and he gave her a bland smile as he reached into his briefcase and retrieved a folder.

'These are the details of the properties I am interested in. Perhaps you could spend some time looking through them this morning, and we can discuss your opinion on their potential suitability over lunch?'

He was too much! 'How about I read through the notes and email you a résumé of my initial thoughts?' she countered, oh-so-politely. 'I don't want to interrupt your schedule.'

Sherry-brown eyes glinted gold with amusement, but the subtle nuance in his tone brooked no argument. 'One o'clock, the Vine, Covent Garden. I expect you to be there, Lauren.' He stood up and extended his hand towards Alistair Gambrill. 'Thank you for your time, Alistair.'

'It's a pleasure to do business with you, Ramon.'

'The pleasure is all mine, I assure you.' There was pure devilment in Ramon's smile as he paused in the doorway and glanced back at Lauren, satisfied to see that she looked flustered and pink-cheeked—and infinitely kissable. But the expression in her eyes made him frown. What had he ever done to cause her to look at him as if she feared him?

She had been on edge from the moment she had walked into Alistair Gambrill's office, he brooded. But perhaps she was simply surprised to see him again after their affair had ended so explosively eighteen months ago. He recalled the ridiculous argument they had had because she had objected when he had referred to her as his mistress. Notoriously hot-tempered, he had reacted to her threat to walk out by telling her that if she did, he would not have her back.

Later, when his temper had cooled and he'd had time to think rationally, he had acknowledged that he had spoken in anger, and he had wondered if Lauren had too. But by then he had returned to

Spain, after a frantic call from his mother telling him that his father's health had deteriorated and that the Duque was gravely ill. Sorting out his personal life had come way down the list of his priorities as he had taken charge of his family.

It was not only business that had brought him back to England, Ramon admitted to himself. He had come because he hoped to persuade Lauren to resume their affair. She was a fiercely independent career woman, and had informed him that she did not want to be his mistress, but he was confident he would be able to convince her that they should be lovers and enjoy an affair for as long as either of them wanted it to last.

He was the Duque de Velaquez, and had a duty to choose a bride from the ranks of Spanish nobility. But he was in no hurry to marry—certainly not until he had got Lauren out of his system, he acknowledged self-derisively. But first he needed to discover why she seemed so wary of him.

CHAPTER TWO

LAUREN arrived at the restaurant at two minutes to one. From his vantage point seated at the bar Ramon watched her slip out of her coat and hand it to the waiter, who had sprung to attendance the moment she walked through the door. Her smile was a killer, he mused. He had never met anyone who could resist its warmth.

Her hair was still swept up into an elegant chignon, and her designer suit and heels were the uniform of a busy professional—a corporate lawyer with a high-flying career. But he remembered the other Lauren. The passionate and sensual woman who had responded to his lovemaking with such sweet eagerness. As she walked towards him Ramon fought the fierce urge to tug the pins from her hair, bury his fingers in the silky mass and hold her captive while he claimed her mouth until she melted against him.

'Ramon.'

He stood up as she reached his side, faintly ir-

ritated that while the waiter had received a smile
he did not. 'As punctual as ever,' he murmured.

'It would be extremely unprofessional to be
late for an appointment with a client,' she replied
crisply.

A subtle reminder that *business* was the only
reason she had agreed to have lunch with him?
Ramon felt a spurt of amusement at Lauren's
determination to put him in his place, but he
also acknowledged a strong desire to shake her
equilibrium.

'Our table is ready.' He paused, and then added
softly, 'It's a pity it's not summer; we could have
eaten outside as we used to. Remember, Lauren?'

Her eyes flew to his face. Of course she remembered, Lauren thought shakily. The memories
of the good times they had shared during their
affair were ingrained in her mind for ever. The
Vine had been one of their favourite haunts, and
they had frequently dined here before returning to
Ramon's penthouse apartment to sate another kind
of hunger. The sex had been urgent, intense, and
unbelievably erotic—a sensual nirvana that was
beyond anything she could ever have imagined.

But it had just been sex. Without strings or the
expectation of commitment or emotion. At least
it had for Ramon, she thought bleakly. For her it
had become something infinitely precious, and

the realisation that she had fallen in love with him was one reason why she had left him.

A waiter led them to their table. 'What would you like to drink?' Ramon enquired when they were seated.

'Iced water, please. And I'd like the Dover sole with new potatoes.' Forgoing a starter and dessert meant that, with luck, lunch should last no longer than thirty minutes.

The waiter departed with their order and she glared across the table. 'What are you playing at, Ramon?'

Dark brows rose slightly at the sharpness of her tone, but he did not immediately reply, instead surveying her flushed face with a speculative gleam in his eyes that lit a flame to her temper.

'Why did you invite me here?' she demanded.

'You know why. I wish to discuss a business venture with my new legal advisor.' He paused, and then added laconically, 'I admit I chose the Vine for purely nostalgic reasons. We shared some good times here.'

'I have no desire to take a trip down memory lane,' she said shortly. 'We've both moved on.'

Ramon stared at Lauren speculatively, aware of the surreptitious glances she had been darting at him. The chemistry was still there, simmering beneath the surface of her cool façade, but the faint tremor of her mouth warned of her determination to fight her awareness of him. For now it was enough to know that he bothered her. He controlled the urge to walk around the table and kiss her into submission, and instead turned his attention to the approaching waiter.

Lauren gave a sigh of relief when their meals were served. The fish was delicious, but she was so acutely conscious of Ramon that her appetite deserted her after a few forkfuls.

'I ran a few preliminary checks on the properties you are interested in, and I can see possible problems with two of them,' she explained, taking the folder of notes from her briefcase. 'The property in Chancery Lane is a Grade II listed building, which means it is of historic interest and you would need to apply for special building consent to do any kind of refurbishment. The property in Jermyn Street has a short lease. I've spoken to the company who own the freehold and have learned that they would consider extending the lease. But obviously that would have to be negotiated.'

Ramon speared his last forkful of steak and savoured it before replying. 'Your efficiency is commendable.'

'That, presumably, is the reason you hired me.'

'One of the reasons.' He met her glare with a bland smile. He'd forgotten how much he enjoyed their verbal sparring, and their conversations about everything from the arts to topical news items.

'Alistair Gambrill thinks highly of you,' he commented. 'Eighteen months ago I remember you had only recently moved to PGH from another law firm, and now I understand that you are being considered for promotion. You must have worked hard to make such a positive impression on the senior partners.'

Lauren threw him a sharp glance, wondering if he was being sarcastic. Her dedication to her job and her refusal to cut down on the long hours she worked had been the only source of friction between them during their affair. Ramon had made it clear that he expected her to be at his beck and call, while she had been infuriated by his chauvinistic attitude and had not held back from telling him so.

He had never understood that her single-minded focus on her career stemmed from an almost obsessive need for financial independence, and a determination never to be reliant on anyone—as her mother had been on her father. But how could he have understood, when she had never told him about her parents' bitter divorce, or that her father had abandoned his family for his mistress and left his wife and daughter virtually penniless?

'The move to PGH has certainly given me an

opportunity to further my career,' she agreed. 'And I work hard at my job.'

He could not know that she felt pressurised to work harder than her contemporaries. Discovering that she was pregnant a month after she had started at PGH had meant that her career had no longer been a choice but a necessity as she faced life as a single mother.

Anxious to prove her worth to Alistair Gambrill and the other senior partners, she had continued to work long hours. Fortunately Mateo's birth had been straightforward, and three months later she had returned to work full-time, afraid that lengthy maternity leave would be detrimental to her chances of promotion in the male-dominated, highly competitive world of corporate law.

She took a sip of water, fiddled restlessly with her napkin, and then said abruptly, 'I'm sorry about your father.' Ramon had always been reluctant to discuss his personal life, and she knew little about his family, but Esteban Velaquez had been a prominent politician in the Spanish government and his death had been reported worldwide.

She did not expect him to comment, and was surprised when, after a long pause, he admitted, 'It was a shock. Cancer had been diagnosed six months earlier, but after surgery his prognosis was good. Unfortunately the disease returned in a more aggressive form and there was nothing more the doctors could do. My mother has taken his death badly,' he continued heavily. 'My parents had been married for over forty years and she is heartbroken.'

His mother's grief had been as much a shock as the loss of his father, Ramon conceded silently. He had assumed that his parents' marriage had been a union between two influential Spanish families—an arrangement that had developed into a contented relationship based on mutual friendship and respect. But after witnessing Marisol Velaquez's raw despair as she wept for her husband he had realised that it had been love that had bound his parents together for almost half a century—the kind of profound and everlasting love that poets wrote sonnets about and which he had cynically doubted existed in real life.

Lauren stared at Ramon's handsome face and felt her stomach dip. He was impossibly gorgeous, but she was not the first woman to be blown away by his sexy good-looks and she certainly would not be the last. Since Esteban Velaquez's death, the press had frequently reported on the playboy lifestyle of his only son and heir. Ramon had been photographed with a number of women—in particular a well-known catwalk model, Pilar Fernandez, who was the daughter of a Spanish aristocrat and whose impeccable pedigree was reflected in her exquisite features. The pictures of Ramon and beautiful Pilar had reinforced Lauren's belief that he would not be interested in his illegitimate child.

'I'm sorry for your mother,' she murmured. 'Perhaps the prospect of you marrying soon will help to alleviate her grief a little? There is speculation in the media that you are about to announce your engagement to Pilar Fernandez,' she added, when his dark brows lifted in silent query.

'I've no doubt my mother would be delighted at the news of my impending nuptials,' he drawled. 'Since my father's death she seems to have made it her life's mission to find me a bride. But the speculation is unfounded. Certain elements of the Spanish press are fascinated with my private life, but Pilar is simply a friend. Our families have known one another for many years. I'm afraid that even for my dear *madre's* sake I am in no hurry to find a *duquesa*.'

His eyes rested deliberately on Lauren's mouth, and the sensual gleam in his eyes sent a quiver of reaction down her spine. His message was loud and clear. Some time in the future he would select a member of the Spanish aristocracy to be his wife and provide him with blue-blooded heirs to continue the Velaquez name, but until then he would enjoy his freedom and satisfy his high sex-drive with numerous mistresses.

But she had been there, done that, Lauren brooded.

Ramon had gone to some lengths to arrange for her to work for him. She recognised the hunger in his eyes, and could feel the undercurrent of sexual tension that had simmered between them since she had walked into the restaurant. It was inconceivable that he wanted to re-ignite their affair when he had insisted eighteen months ago that if she left him he would never take her back. But if that *was* his intention—dear heaven, she thought shakily—she could only pray she had the strength to resist him.

Tension tightened its grip on her. She could not allow him to find out about Matty. He would surely not deem her son a suitable heir for a family who could trace its ancestors back to the eleventh century, when Rioja had been fought over by the ancient kingdoms of Castile and Navarre. Matty was her baby, her responsibility, and it would be better for everyone if he remained her secret.

The arrival of the waiter dragged her mind back to her surroundings. 'Would you like dessert?' Ramon asked.

'No, thanks.' Her hands were trembling as she shoved the notes on the properties back in her briefcase. 'I should go. I need to get back to the office to hand over the accounts on my file to other lawyers in the department.'

'I'm sure they can wait another fifteen minutes,' he said dryly before he turned to the waiter, 'An Americano, please, and a jasmine tea.'

Did it mean anything that he remembered she always liked to end a meal with cup of herbal tea? All it proved was that he had a good memory, Lauren told herself firmly.

The waiter returned with their beverages and she sipped her fragrant tea.

'So, what has been happening in your life since we split up?' Ramon queried in a casual tone, the intent expression in his eyes shadowed by his thick lashes. 'Is there anyone special in your life, Lauren?'

Only her son, who filled her life so completely that there was no room for anyone else—but she could not tell Ramon that, and gave a noncommittal shrug. 'I don't think that's any of your business.'

So there *was* some guy. It was hardly surprising, Ramon conceded. Lauren was a beautiful, sensual woman, and she would not have spent the past eighteen months alone. What *was* surprising was how much he disliked the idea of her with a lover.

He leaned back in his chair and studied her broodingly. 'I feel sorry for this guy, whoever he is.'

'What?' It took a few seconds for it to sink in that Ramon believed she was dating someone. Lauren frowned. 'Why?'

'Because he doesn't satisfy you.'

'Oh? You know that, do you?' She had forgotten how infuriatingly arrogant he could be.

'I can tell.' He moved so suddenly that she had no time to react as he leaned across the table and captured her chin in his hand. 'If lover-boy satisfied you, your eyes wouldn't darken to the colour of woodsmoke when you look at me.' He ran his thumb pad over her lower lip and felt its betraying tremble. 'And your mouth wouldn't soften in readiness for my kiss.'

'It doesn't… I don't…' Shaking with anger, and another emotion she refused to define, Lauren jumped to her feet so abruptly that her chair toppled over and hit the floor with a clatter that drew curious glances from around the restaurant.

The noise brought her to her senses and she snatched a breath, willing herself to act with calm dignity even though her heart was pounding.

'I don't know what game you're playing,' she said coldly, 'but perhaps I should remind you that I ended our affair a year and a half ago. You might have employed me to work for you, but I expect our relationship to be conducted on a purely professional level, with no references to my private life and no…'

'Kissing?' Ramon suggested dulcetly.

His teasing smile tugged on her heart. She had forgotten his wicked sense of humour, and how often he had made her laugh, and for some inexplicable reason tears stung her eyes.

'You are insufferable,' she hissed, suddenly aware that the waiter, who had hurried over to pick up her chair, was clearly intrigued by their conversation. 'I'm going back to work.'

'I'll take you,' Ramon handed the waiter his credit card to settle the bill. 'After I've shown you where you'll be based while you are working for me.'

Lauren knew enough about cars to recognise that Ramon's sleek silver Porsche was a top-of-the-range model. As she slid into the passenger seat she felt a little pang of regret for her beloved red sports car, which she had traded in for a family saloon big enough to fit in Mateo's baby seat and the mountain of other paraphernalia required for one small child.

Her life was so different now, she brooded. She was no longer a carefree young woman, swept up in the excitement of a passionate affair with a sexy Spanish playboy. Now she was a mother, with all the responsibilities that entailed. But she wouldn't have it any other way. Matty was her life; and the highlight of her day was when she picked him up from the daycare nursery and he wrapped his chubby arms around her neck and smothered her face in wet kisses.

Lost in her thoughts, she did not pay any attention to the route Ramon was taking through the congested London streets until they neared Marble Arch and swung into Park Lane.

'Why are we here?' she asked him with a frown when he drove through a gateway and down a ramp which led to an underground car park. She recognised the place instantly. Eighteen months ago she had often stayed at Ramon's luxurious penthouse apartment, but she could not understand why he was taking her there now.

'I have my offices here.' He parked, climbed out of the car and walked around to open her door.

Lauren followed him into the lift, her heart suddenly beating painfully fast as she remembered all the occasions when Ramon had pulled her into his arms and kissed her until they had reached the top floor, dispensing with her clothes, his, the moment they reached his apartment, sometimes making it to the bedroom, sometimes only getting as far as the sitting room sofa, before their hunger for each other overwhelmed them.

The image of his muscular naked body descending slowly onto hers, his powerful erection penetrating her inch by glorious inch, was so vivid that she closed her eyes, terrified he would guess her wayward thoughts. She could sense his intent scrutiny but refused to meet his gaze, and bit down hard on her lip when he stood aside for her to precede him out of the lift.

'Are your offices up here?' She glanced along the corridor, frowning as she searched for a door other than the one that she knew led into the penthouse.

'Uh-huh.' Ramon slotted a card into the door security system and ushered her inside. The apartment was achingly familiar—a wide hallway, with various spacious rooms leading off it, all decorated in neutral shades and furnished with contemporary pieces which provided splashes of bold colour. Through a half-open door Lauren could see the master bedroom. Memories crowded in on her and she halted abruptly, gripped by sudden panic.

'Is this is another one of your games?' she demanded sharply. 'You said you were going to show me my office.'

Ramon gave her a musing look, taking in her flushed face and the slight tremor of her mouth.

This wasn't the first time she had seemed uneasy with him, and he was intrigued to know what was bothering her.

'It's in here.' He pushed open a door at the far end of the hall and led the way into a room which Lauren remembered had once been a small sitting room. It now housed a desk, computer, and other office furniture. 'I'm working from my study, adjoining this room, until I can rent a suitable office complex for the London subsidiary of Velaquez Conglomerates,' he told her. 'In fact, that will be your first task. I recently viewed a new commercial building at St Katherine's Dock, and I want you to deal with the lease contract.'

When Lauren made no reply he continued, 'My PA has remained in Spain, and I'm using secretarial staff from a temp agency until I find a permanent base. Sally comes here a couple of mornings a week so that I can dictate correspondence.'

So working from the apartment would only be a temporary arrangement, Lauren tried to reassure herself. But it could still take weeks, maybe months, before Velaquez Conglomerates took over the new offices—which meant that she would have to come here every day and re-live memories of all the times Ramon had made love to her. Dear heaven—Mateo had been conceived here!

She had walked across to the window, to stare at the view over Hyde Park, but now she swung round to face him, her body rigid with tension. 'This isn't going to work,' she said tersely. 'It's easier for me to commute from PGH's offices than here. I can be in constant communication with you by email or phone…'

Ramon shook his head. 'I'd prefer you to be here.'

'*Why?*' she cried, unable to control her emotions any longer. She had been so shocked to see him again, and coming back to the apartment where they had been lovers was sheer agony. Throughout lunch she had felt as though he was stripping away her protective shell, layer by layer, and she was terrified that if she didn't leave now he was going to guess how much he affected her.

Ramon's eyes had narrowed at her outburst, and now he strolled towards her, as silent and intent as a panther stalking its prey, and twice as deadly. The atmosphere shifted subtly, the tension between them so tangible that Lauren's skin prickled.

'What exactly are you worried about, Lauren?' he asked softly.

'I'm not worried about anything,' she denied desperately, sure he must hear her heart hammering against her ribs. He was too big, too close, and memories of his demanding mouth plundering hers hurt too much. 'I simply don't understand what all this is about, Ramon. Why you've gone to such lengths to manipulate me into working for you.'

He said nothing, just kept on coming towards her, and the stark hunger in his eyes robbed her of breath. 'What do you want from me?' she whispered, and her heart stopped when his hand shot out to cup her nape and his head slowly descended.

'I want this, *querida*,' he said harshly, and covered her mouth with his own.

CHAPTER THREE

LAUREN'S lips parted to voice her protest, but the words were lost beneath the bruising pressure of Ramon's mouth. The kiss was no gentle seduction, but a hot, hungry ravishment of her senses as he took without mercy, demanding a response she was powerless to deny.

Sexual tension had smouldered between them since he had walked into Alistair Gambrill's office, and now it exploded in a firestorm of passion. She was vaguely aware of his hand moving up from her nape, and felt him release the clip that secured her chignon so that her hair fell around her shoulders in a fragrant, silky curtain.

She should stop him, insisted the voice of reason in her head. But the bold thrust of his tongue into her mouth drove everything from her mind but her need for him to keep on kissing her and never stop. It had been so long since she had been held in his arms, and acting purely on instinct she pressed closer to him, so that her soft breasts were crushed against the solid wall of his chest.

'Querida.'

The gravelly sexiness of his voice made her tremble. She had placed her hands on his chest to push him away, but now they crept of their own accord to his shoulders as he freed the buttons of her jacket and pushed the material aside, so that he could cup her breast in his palm.

His hand felt deliciously warm through the fine silk of her blouse, and she caught her breath when he stroked his thumb-pad lightly over her nipple so that it tightened and strained against the sheer fabric of her bra. She wanted more, Lauren acknowledged restlessly. She wanted to feel his naked flesh on hers. Her fingers tugged urgently on his shirt buttons, her breathing fractured as she stroked her hands over the intoxicating warmth of his satiny skin and felt the faint abrasion of the crisp dark hairs that covered his chest.

It was as if she had hurtled back in time, and the months that they had been apart had never happened. When they had become lovers Ramon had unlocked her sensuality, and only he had the key. Her breasts felt heavy, and she was aware of a betraying dampness between her legs as she felt the hard ridge of his arousal nudge against her pelvis. And all the time he continued to kiss her, slow and deep now, and so incredibly sensual that a low moan rose in her throat.

Satisfaction swept through Ramon when he felt Lauren melt against him. He hadn't planned for things to get this out of hand—not yet—but it seemed that she shared his urgent need to rediscover the sexual ecstasy that he knew without doubt he would experience with her.

With deft fingers he unbuttoned her blouse, and groaned as he slipped his hand inside her bra and rolled her swollen nipple between his finger and thumb. He felt the tremor that shook her, and suddenly his patience snapped. He wanted her now—hard and fast across the desk—and with a muttered oath he thrust his other hand beneath the hem of her skirt and skimmed his fingers over her gossamer-fine hose, the wide band of lace at the top of her stocking, and finally the silky-smooth flesh of her inner thigh.

'*Dios mio, querida*—I have to have you now.'

Oh, please, yes—now, *now*. The words were like a chant in Lauren's head. She hadn't felt sexual desire for so long. It was as if those feelings had been locked away since she had ended her affair with Ramon. But now he was here, and her body was screaming for the fulfilment only he could give. The feel of his hand on her thigh was unbearably frustrating when she longed for him to move it higher and slip it beneath the edge of her knickers, to touch her where he hadn't touched her for so long.

She could sense his impatience, and the thought filtered into her mind that she hoped he would be gentle. Mateo's birth had been relatively short, but nonetheless it had been a painful experience...

Matty!

She tensed, and her eyes flew open as reality doused her in an ice-cold shower. *What in heaven's name was she doing?*

For a few seconds she was torn between the powerful drumbeat of her desire and the firm insistence of her brain, that told her she must stop this *now*—because allowing Ramon to make love to her would only make an already complicated situation even worse.

'*No!*' Her sharp denial sliced through the air, and, taking advantage of Ramon's surprise, she pulled out of his arms and stood shaking like a leaf in a storm as she frantically refastened her blouse.

'No?'

His tone was deceptively soft, but she could sense his anger. It was justified when she had responded to him with such wanton enthusiasm, she thought miserably. She had given him every reason to believe that she was happy to leap into bed with him, but thoughts of Mateo had brought her crashing back to earth. She could not make love with Ramon when she had kept his son a secret from him.

Ramon drew a harsh breath as he fought the urge to snatch Lauren back into his arms and finish what they had started. Frustration clawed in his gut and made him want to lash out.

'We both know how easily I could make you change your mind,' he taunted. He stared at her nipples, jutting so provocatively through her blouse, and cursed the throbbing ache in his groin. 'You say no, but your body says yes, *querida*.'

'Well, it's been outvoted,' Lauren bit out, barely trusting herself to speak as she struggled to regain some sense of composure. 'You…you took me by surprise, but I don't want you, Ramon.'

'Are you sure about that?' Ramon demanded disbelievingly. 'I've just proved that the fire still burns for both of us.' She had tormented his thoughts and disturbed his dreams for months, until he had given in to his need to find her again. 'I want you back, Lauren,' he admitted roughly.

His voice had softened, and when Lauren stared into his sherry-brown eyes that were so like Matty's her heart ached. His words were beguiling. Perhaps it was being back here at his apartment, where they had shared so many good times, that was undermining her defences, but Ramon had sounded serious. Did he mean that he wanted a proper, meaningful relationship with her? she wondered, clutching at the fragile green shoot of hope. And, if so, would he want Mateo too? Was there the slightest possibility that they could work things out?

'I thought you were supposed to marry a woman from the Spanish nobility who would give you an heir to continue the Velaquez name?' she said shakily. 'Are you saying the situation has changed?'

Ramon shrugged. 'No. It is still my intention to fulfil my duty. But that is for the future. For now I want to concentrate on running Velaquez Conglomerates and the Castillo del Toro. I do not wish to have a child yet, and therefore I do not need to consider marriage for several years.' He paused, and deliberately dropped his gaze to her breasts. 'But neither do I have any wish to live like a monk, *querida*,' he drawled softly.

Lauren cursed her body's traitorous reaction to the hungry gleam in his eyes. So all he wanted was an affair. The little shoot of hope shrivelled and died. Nothing had changed, she thought painfully. She wondered if he realised how insulted she felt to be told that he only considered her good enough to be his mistress, but not his wife.

Admittedly marriage was not something *she* wanted, she thought wearily, rubbing her brow as myriad confused thoughts swirled inside her head. Having witnessed her mother's devastation after her father had walked out, she had decided that she would never give up her independence for any man.

Plenty of couples lived together without being legally bound in a relationship. But Ramon was not even suggesting a long-term commitment, she thought dully. He simply wanted her in his bed for a month or two—until he grew tired of her. Perhaps if she'd only had herself to consider she might be tempted to bury her pride and accept his offer. Eighteen months ago he had stolen her heart, and she longed to recapture the fun and laughter and the long nights of tender lovemaking that they had shared during their affair. But there was not only herself—there was Matty. And Ramon had stated that he did not want a child yet. She wasn't sure he would *ever* want a child born to his English mistress.

Her conscience prickled. She had never given Ramon the chance to show how he would react to the news that he had a son. But everything he had said a few moments ago reinforced her belief that he would not want Matty. His strong sense of duty might compel him to offer financial support for his child, but, as she knew only too well, a child needed to feel loved and cherished, and she feared that Matty would find a monthly maintenance cheque a poor substitute for a father.

She dragged her gaze from the sight of him refastening his shirt, blushing when she recalled how she had wrenched the buttons open in her feverish need to touch his naked skin.

'It would be inappropriate for me to have an affair with you,' she told him stiffly. 'You are a client of PGH, and you must see it would be highly unprofessional.' She walked over to the door, praying that she appeared more in control of herself than she felt. 'For that reason I think it would be best if you chose another lawyer from the commercial property department to work on your project. There are a number of excellent lawyers at PGH who would be delighted to work for Velaquez Conglomerates.'

Guy Hadlow would seize the chance, she thought dismally. She would have to make the excuse to Alistair Gambrill that she did not feel capable of taking on the Velaquez project because of personal commitments. It would almost certainly ruin her chances of promotion, but she could not work with Ramon now that she knew he wanted her back in his bed.

'I'll speak to Alistair.' She opened the door, and

was about to step into the hallway when Ramon's voice halted her.

'How do you suppose Alistair Gambrill will take the news that I am cancelling the Velaquez contract with PGH?' he drawled.

'You're not.' Startled, Lauren swung back to face him, imagining with horror the senior partner's reaction if he learned that the lucrative contact with Velaquez Conglomerates would not go ahead. 'I mean, there's no need for that. I've explained. There are other commercial property lawyers…'

'I want *you*.' His expression was unfathomable, but something in his voice warned Lauren that his threat to cancel the contract with PGH was deadly serious. 'I will respect your position as my legal advisor and there will be no other relationship between us—unless you wish there to be.'

'I don't,' she snapped.

He ignored her interruption and continued smoothly, 'My decision to use PGH only stands if you agree to act as my lawyer on the wine bar project. If you refuse then I will find another law firm—which I am sure that both you and Alistair Gambrill would prefer not to happen,' he added, with a gently mocking smile.

If she was deemed responsible for the loss of a highly influential client her career would suffer irreparable damage at PGH, and probably with other law firms, Lauren thought sickly. Senior lawyers were a tight clique. Doubts about her professional ability would spread, and she would find it hard to get another job in the City.

She stared at Ramon's hard face and her heart sank. 'That's blackmail.'

He lifted his shoulders laconically, utterly unconcerned by her accusation. 'You should know by now that I always get what I want.'

Oh, yes, she knew all right, Lauren brooded bitterly. Ramon's reputation as a ruthlessness businessman was legendary. She had no option but to work for him, but if he thought she was going to fall into his bed because he had decided that he wanted her back as his mistress he had better think again.

'Doesn't it bother you to know that you'll be working with someone who dislikes you intensely?' she said tightly.

'No.' His arrogant smile caused her to grind her teeth. 'But I have to say I'm surprised that someone who dislikes me as much as you say you do could have responded to me with such passion a few minutes ago. Perhaps you don't know what you want, *querida*?' he suggested softly.

While she struggled to formulate a reply, he strolled over to the desk and opened a file.

'These are the details of the office complex in St Katherine's Dock. I'd like you to start work on the lease agreement straight away. If you're staying, that is?' he added, when she continued to hover uncertainly in the doorway.

With as much dignity as she could muster Lauren marched back across the room, sat down at the desk, and immediately focused her attention on the pile of documents, her silence thrumming with fury.

Ramon resisted the urge to brush a tendril of hair off her face, and dropped her hairclip on the desk. 'I guess you want this back.'

'Thank you.' Her voice dripped ice.

He watched her scrape her hair back and clip the honey-gold mass on top of her head, and tried to ignore the sharp tug of desire in his gut. 'I have a couple of meetings booked for this afternoon, and I probably won't be back until late.'

'Then it's likely I'll have left by the time you return.' Lauren lifted her head and met his gaze steadily. 'I finish at the office at five-thirty. That's non-negotiable. But I'm happy to take work home to complete in the evenings if necessary.'

Ramon's eyes narrowed, his curiosity aroused by the quiet determination in her voice. 'Everything is negotiable, Lauren.'

'Not this.' She collected Mateo from the day

nursery at six-fifteen every evening, and not even the threat of losing her job would persuade her to work late.

'I remember that you frequently used to work until seven or eight p.m.' Ramon paused. 'Maybe there's someone you rush home to?'

He was skating dangerously near the truth. She flushed, and tore her eyes from his to stare down at the papers in front of her. 'We've already established that my personal life is not your concern.'

'Oh, we've established a number of things,' Ramon drawled in a dangerously soft voice. 'Not least that you are hot for me—much as you want to deny it.'

Lauren's face burned, and she cursed those moments of weakness when she had responded to his kiss with a hunger that had more than matched his own. 'As a matter of fact I need to leave half an hour earlier tonight. My mother is arriving from Jersey, and I've arranged to meet her at Gatwick.' She hesitated. 'I've already asked Alistair Gambrill for the time off. I hope it's all right with you.'

Ramon gave her a sardonic look. 'It will have to be, won't it?' He paused and studied her speculatively. 'Is there anything else you should tell me?'

Her heart almost leapt out of her chest, and her eyes flew to his face. Did he mean Matty? Did he know…? His expression was unfathomable. 'Wh…what do you mean?' she stammered.

'I simply wondered if you had any other engagements booked that I should know about, so that I can arrange viewings of properties around any other commitments you might have.' Ramon stared at her impatiently. 'Why are you so edgy, Lauren? And why do I get the impression that you're hiding something from me?'

Her palms felt clammy, and it took all her willpower to meet his gaze. 'I really don't know where you would get such a ridiculous idea from,' she said, managing to sound coolly dismissive. 'I'm not hiding anything.'

'Liar. You are doing your best to hide the fact that you are still attracted to me.' Ramon suddenly leaned forward, rested one hand on the desk, and placed the other on her nape. 'But you are not succeeding. Your eyes give you away, *querida*,' he drawled, before he swooped and captured her mouth in a brief, hard kiss that left her aching for more.

He smiled sardonically at the confused mixture of anger and desire in her eyes, and then released her and strolled across to the door. 'I'll see you later,' he threw over his shoulder—leaving Lauren too emotionally drained to wonder why he had said *later* rather than on Monday.

* * *

'I'm sure Mateo will be walking before he's a year old. Look how well he's balancing on his feet.'

Lauren glanced up from her laptop and smiled at the sight of her mother, kneeling on the floor playing with Matty. 'Do you think he's advanced for his age?'

'Goodness, yes.' Frances Maitland beamed at her little grandson. 'You were such a cautious baby—you didn't even crawl until you were eleven months—but he's so active. He certainly doesn't get his daring nature from you. He must have inherited it from his fa—' She stopped abruptly and looked flustered.

'From his father,' Lauren finished her mother's sentence dryly. 'You *can* say the word you know, Mum.'

'Well, it seems strange to talk about Matty's father when I don't even know his name,' Frances muttered. 'I wish you would tell me about him. I don't know why it's all so secret.'

Lauren stifled a sigh. 'I *have* told you about him. He's a playboy. We had a brief affair, but when I found out I was pregnant I knew he wouldn't want a child, so I didn't tell him. End of story.'

Frances sniffed. 'It's not right that you have to work so hard to support Matty on your own. You must be entitled to maintenance from his father.'

Lauren shook her head fiercely. 'I would never

demand money for my son. Mateo is my responsibility, and I can give him everything he needs.' She watched the baby zooming around the carpet on his hands and knees and frowned. 'I still think he looks a bit flushed. And it's strange that he didn't eat his tea. Usually he loves his food. I don't think I'll go to the party tonight, in case he's coming down with something.'

Frances stood up and lifted the chuckling baby into her arms. 'He's absolutely fine. You can't miss the Valentine's Ball—I thought it was PGH's big social event of the year?'

'It is,' Lauren said heavily.

Alistair Gambrill's wife organised the ball each year, and a proportion of the ticket money was donated to charity. The law firm's most prestigious clients were invited, and every member of staff was expected to attend—particularly those who were chasing a promotion, she thought ruefully. She was still reeling from the shock of seeing Ramon again today, and felt in no mood to socialise, but she knew her absence would be noted by the senior partners.

'Well, maybe I'll go, but then come home tonight,' she muttered. The ball was held in a hotel, and the ticket included overnight accommodation so that guests could drink and not have to worry about driving.

'It's one night, for goodness' sake,' Frances said impatiently. 'Don't you trust me to look after my grandson for one night?'

'Of course I do, but—' Lauren broke off help-lessly when she saw the light of battle in her moth-er's eyes. Mateo's flushed cheeks were probably because it was warm in the flat. He looked the picture of health, with his bright eyes and cheeky grin, and she knew Frances had been looking for-ward to spending some time with him. 'All right.' She gave in. 'I'll go.'

'Good.' Frances beamed. 'You never know— you might be swept off your feet by a handsome stranger.'

'God forbid!' Lauren said fervently as she pressed the 'send' button on her laptop to email the report she had been working on to Ramon. 'The expression "once bitten, twice shy" has never been more apt.'

Huge, ornate chandeliers illuminated the ballroom and sparkled down on the dozens of guests who were milling about the room. Lauren smiled her thanks to the waiter who offered her a glass of champagne, and smoothed her hand down her dress as she made her way towards the group of senior partners and their wives. Her floor-length black silk-jersey gown was simple but elegant; the diamanté shoulder straps and narrow belt around her waist broke the starkness of the dress, and matched her silver stiletto heels.

It was amazing to think that ten months ago she had looked like a barrage balloon in full flight, she mused when she caught sight of her reflection in a mirror. She was lucky that her stomach had regained its pre-pregnancy flatness, but she had eaten sensibly while she was expecting Mateo, and, thanks to her hectic life of combining work and motherhood, she was actually a few pounds lighter than before she had conceived him.

It made a change to dress up for once, she admitted, feeling a little spurt of confidence when she became aware of the admiring glances from a couple of lawyers from another department of PGH. She continued on her way over to the senior partners, but her steps faltered, and for the second time that day shock drained the blood from her face as she caught sight of a familiar tall, dark figure.

What in the devil's name was Ramon doing here?

'Ah, Lauren, delighted you could make it.' Alistair Gambrill chose that moment to turn his head in her direction, so she had no option but to carry on walking, her heart thudding painfully as she felt Ramon's intent scrutiny.

'Good evening.' She managed a brittle smile for Alistair and the other partners, and somehow forced herself to meet Ramon's glinting gaze.

'You and Ramon have met, of course.' Alistair gave her a faint frown. 'Actually, I was surprised you hadn't invited Ramon tonight. I'm sure you are aware that PGH are always delighted to welcome clients to our Valentine's Ball.'

'I…' Hot colour stormed back into Lauren's face.

'As a matter of fact, Lauren did issue an invitation,' Ramon murmured smoothly. 'I had to decline because of a prior engagement, but that engagement was cancelled just before you telephoned me, Alistair, so I was able to attend the ball after all.'

'Ah, well. Good!' Alistair's face cleared and he gave a jovial smile. 'Ramon was just saying that he is new to London and isn't acquainted with any of the other guests here tonight. I know you'll be delighted to introduce him to people, won't you, Lauren?'

'Delighted,' she assured the senior partner through gritted teeth. She knew she should be grateful to Ramon for covering up her lapse in not inviting him to the ball, but he knew of course that she had deliberately not done so, and his smug smile was infuriating.

'I will certainly appreciate your company,' Ramon assured her, pure devilment gleaming in his eyes. 'Allow me to get you another drink.'

'New to London!' she snorted, stalking furiously beside him when he took her elbow and guided her towards the bar. 'Presumably Alistair is unaware that you've slept with just about every woman in the capital between the ages of eighteen and sixty?' She glared at him when he chuckled, the sound of his sexy laugh causing a squirming sensation in the pit of her stomach. 'Would you like me to hold your hand while I introduce you around?' she queried sarcastically.

'To be honest, I would prefer you to hold another area of my anatomy, *querida*,' he said dulcetly. 'But as we are in public I will settle for your hand in mine.'

'How dare you...?' Scarlet-cheeked, Lauren tried to snatch her hand from his grasp, but with insulting ease he tugged her onto the dance floor and settled his other hand on her hip, the mocking glint in his eyes warning her that she would come off worst if she caused a scene.

'Relax,' he bade her, his breath whispering against her ear as he drew her rigid body closer against his broad chest. 'You used to enjoy dancing with me.'

But that had been back in the heady days of their

affair, when she had kidded herself that he saw her as more than a convenient mistress, Lauren thought bleakly. Now she knew that she could never mean anything to him.

But trying to disguise her intense awareness of him was not her only problem. Far more seriously, most of the PHG staff knew she had a child, and it would only take one unwitting remark to alert Ramon to that fact. Panic surged through her. Perhaps it would be better if she danced with him all night, she thought wildly. At least that way he could not speak to anyone else.

Ramon inhaled the lemony scent of Lauren's hair, and could not resist sliding his hand up her back to tangle his fingers in the long honey-blonde tresses that she had left loose tonight. *Dios*, she was beautiful. And soon she would be his again, and he would slide his hands not over her dress but across her naked satin-soft skin. He moved his hand down to her *derrière*, and felt the tremor that ran through her when he drew her hard against the throbbing erection straining beneath his trousers. For a second he almost gave in to the temptation to scoop her up and stride out of the ballroom, up to his hotel room, but he forced himself to be patient and bide his time.

'How about that drink?' he murmured, a long while later.

Lauren lifted her head from Ramon's chest and stared at him dazedly, appalled that she had been so seduced by the warmth of his body that she had melted against him. She had no idea how long they had been dancing. All she had been aware of was the sensual, spicy scent of his cologne and the steady thud of his heart beneath her ear.

The heartbeat was such a poignant sound—the drumbeat of life, she thought emotively. When she had been pregnant, hearing her baby's heartbeat on the monitor at her antenatal appointments had been so exciting. It had been a link with her child—a link that Ramon had never experienced, because she had never told him that she had conceived his baby.

She bit her lip and tore her gaze from the golden-brown eyes that were so like Matty's. Had she been wrong to deny him his child? she wondered desperately. It was a question that had haunted her constantly over the past months. She had tried to do the right thing for Matty—had been so afraid that Ramon would not love her baby that she had decided to bring him up on her own. But what if that decision had been wrong? Supposing Ramon would have loved Matty even if he was not the noble heir deemed necessary for the Duque de Velaquez?

Her thoughts swirled in her head until she felt as

though her skull was about to split open. Unable to meet Ramon's gaze, she glanced around the ballroom and realised that many of her work colleagues were staring at her speculatively. Their curiosity was not surprising, since she *had* been snuggled up to PGH's most prestigious client, she acknowledged grimly. Guy Hadlow was leaning against a pillar, watching her, and his knowing smirk was mortifying.

'I seem to have monopolised your attention for far too long,' she said stiffly.

'I'm not complaining, *querida*.' Ramon's confident smile held it all—satisfaction that she had succumbed to his potent charm, and the expectation that he had only to click his fingers and she would fall into his bed.

She had to get away from him before she made an even bigger fool of herself. 'Actually, I've got a headache. Please excuse me,' she mumbled, and spun away from him before he had a chance to protest.

She walked swiftly across the ballroom, needing to escape the cacophony of noise, the sound of people's voices and the music. She needed to be alone, to think, as the enormity of her decision to keep Matty a secret from Ramon evoked the nagging guilt that she had tried to push away.

She hurried into the lift and pressed the button

to take her to the fifth floor. The door had started to close when a figure appeared, and she gave a silent groan when Guy Hadlow joined her.

'Off to bed so early, Lauren?' he taunted.

She ignored him, but he moved closer, trapping her against the wall of the lift. She wrinkled her nose in distaste when she inhaled the strong smell of alcohol on his breath.

'The question is—whose bed? Are you going to bunk up with your Spanish playboy?' Guy gave a mocking laugh. 'No wonder you were picked for the Velaquez job. What did you do? Promise to drop your knickers if he gave you the contract?'

The crack of Lauren's hand on Guy's cheek resounded around the lift and he jerked his head back, his mouth thinning to an ugly line.

'You bitch. I'm only saying what everyone is thinking.'

'Well, it's not true.' Lauren felt sick with shame and misery. She heard the ping of the bell announcing that the lift had arrived at her floor and tried to push past Guy—but he gripped her arms with bruising force.

'Really? You give it away for free, do you, Lauren?' the lawyer sneered nastily.

To her horror he hit the button to prevent the lift door from opening. She could tell from his flushed face and glazed eyes that he was seriously drunk, but while she was desperately searching for something to say that would defuse the situation he grabbed one strap of her dress and wrenched it down over her shoulder.

'For God's sake, Guy, let me go.' She could hear the panic in her voice, and shuddered when he lowered his head towards her.

'I wanted you long before Velaquez,' he slurred.

Nausea swept through Lauren when he put his hand on her breast, but she quickly took advantage of the fact that he had released his grip on her arm, and somehow found the strength to push him away. The lift was still stationary. She frantically jabbed the button to open the door, and stumbled blindly out into the corridor—straight into the solid wall of a broad, muscular chest.

CHAPTER FOUR

'LAUREN? What's going on?'

Ramon stared down at Lauren's paper-white face, and the purple bruises already appearing on her upper arms, then swung his gaze to the man still lounging against the lift wall. He had felt a faint sense of unease when he had watched the man follow her into the lift a few minutes ago, and had quickly taken the other lift up to the fifth floor. It seemed that his instincts had been right, he thought grimly.

Lauren shook her head, beyond speech. She was sure she had been in no real danger from Guy, but the memory of his sweaty hands on her skin as he had pawed her made her sway on her feet.

She could have no idea how vulnerable she looked at this moment, Ramon thought savagely, white-hot fury surging through him. He was startled by the strength of his need to protect her. He wanted to take her in his arms and simply hold her—let her know she was safe with him and that he would never allow anyone to harm her—but first he had to deal with the jerk in the lift.

'Just a moment, *querida*,' he said, as he gently moved Lauren to one side. 'Let me get rid of this trash.'

'Ramon, what are you doing?' Lauren gasped, when Ramon grabbed Guy by the lapels of his jacket and raised his fist. '*No!* You can't hit him. He's drunk.'

'And that's his defence?' Ramon growled. 'He hurt you.'

Guy's bravado had deflated like a popped balloon, and he cowered away from the furious Spaniard. 'He was just being an idiot,' Lauren said heavily. She still felt sick when she remembered how Guy had dragged the strap of her dress down her arm, but it was obvious he had had too much to drink. 'Look at him; he can hardly stand up. Anyway, brawling with him will only make everything a hundred times worse.'

Ramon frowned, but reluctantly released Guy. 'Go and sober up,' he ordered the younger man harshly, 'and if you value your life keep away from Miss Maitland in the future.'

Guy did not argue as he stumbled out of the lift and almost ran along the corridor. Lauren hugged her arms around herself, shivering as shock set in.

'Here.' Ramon slipped off his jacket and draped it around her shoulders.

The silk lining was warm, and carried the faint scent of his cologne. Lauren hugged it to her as he guided her back into the lift. 'That was my floor,' she muttered, her brain finally clicking into gear when the lift moved smoothly upwards. 'Where are we going?'

'You need a drink, and I have a bottle of brandy in my room—unless you want to go back downstairs to the bar?' he suggested, when she looked as though she was about to argue.

Lauren shuddered at the thought of returning to the party with Ramon, knowing they would attract curious glances from the other PGH staff. But she could not risk being alone with him, she thought desperately. Not because she feared him in any way. No—it was herself, and her overwhelming awareness of him that scared the life out of her.

But when the lift halted at the top floor it was easier to follow him down the corridor than to cause a scene—especially as her legs suddenly felt as though they were about to give way beneath her. Unlike her small, functional hotel room, Ramon's suite was large and luxurious, and she sank down onto one of the leather sofas while he crossed to the bar and poured them both a drink.

'Here—drink this. It might bring some colour back to your face.'

She was about to remind him that she never drank alcohol, but the expression in his eyes warned her that his patience was dangerously thin, so she obediently took a sip of brandy and winced when it burned the back of her throat.

Ramon dropped down onto the sofa beside her, close enough that she was aware of the heat emanating from his body. He loosened his bow-tie and unfastened the top couple of shirt buttons to reveal several inches of olive-gold skin and a sprinkling of dark chest hairs. After one furtive glance at him, Lauren took another gulp of brandy.

'So what was all that about?' His eyes darkened as he inspected the bruises on her arms. 'You should have let me hit the bastard.'

'Guy was just being…Guy. He's asked me out a few times in the past, and didn't like it when I turned him down. Anyway, maybe he has a point,' Lauren said dully, feeling another wave of sick misery wash over her when she remembered Guy's remarks about the reason she had been given the Velaquez contract.

Ramon frowned. What do you mean?'

'I mean that, according to Guy, everyone at PGH thinks you picked me to work for you for other reasons than my capabilities as a lawyer,' she said bitterly. 'There are several other commercial property lawyers who are more qualified and experienced than me, so I suppose it's not surprising that people believe I slept my way into the job.'

'As a matter of fact Alistair Gambrill recommended that you would be the best person to work on my project,' Ramon told her quietly.

The knowledge made her feel marginally better. 'But you know what office gossip is like,' she burst out, jumping to her feet in agitation. 'People will have been wondering why I was chosen for the contract above more senior lawyers, and the fact that you danced with me all evening will fuel the rumours about me.'

Anger and humiliation surged up inside her, and she spun round to face Ramon, her eyes flashing fire. 'I'll be known as the Mata Hari of the legal world,' she cried wildly, 'and it's all your fault.' Once again he had turned her world upside down. 'Why did you have to come back, Ramon?'

'Because I couldn't keep away,' he countered harshly. He stood up, his eyes fixed intently on her, and the blazing fire in their golden depths sent an answering heat coursing through her veins. 'I tried to forget you—but, *Dios*! You were always there in my mind. Even on the day of my father's funeral I found myself thinking about you,' he revealed grimly, his voice laced with self-disgust, because in the midst of his grief he had closed his eyes and imagined himself resting his head on Lauren's breasts. Of course he had not wanted to be comforted by her, he told himself angrily. He had wanted sex: the physical satisfaction that for some reason was so much more intense with her than with any other woman.

She should move, Lauren told herself as Ramon strode towards her. She should run for the door and keep on running. But her feet seemed to be welded to the floor, and her heart was beating so fast that her breath came in sharp little gasps.

He was so close that she could see the flecks of gold in his eyes, and a rampant, undisguised sexual hunger that filled her with fear and shameful longing. 'Leave me alone,' she said shakily, putting out a hand to ward him off.

He laughed and caught hold of her, dragging her up against his hard, aroused body. 'Oh, *querida*, I would if I thought for one minute you meant it. But your body gives you away—see?' He curved his hand possessively around her breast, his smile mocking as he stroked his thumb lightly across her nipple and it instantly swelled and jutted against the sheer fabric of her dress.

Why couldn't she feel the same disgust she had felt when Guy had touched her? Lauren asked herself despairingly. But Ramon was no clumsy, drunken boor. He was a highly skilled lover, with a wealth of experience in the art of sex. More than that, he was the man who had stolen her heart, her one love, she acknowledged silently, unable to tear her eyes from his as he slowly lowered his head.

She had expected his kiss to be hard and demanding—a demonstration of his power over her. But the gossamer-soft brush of his lips across hers was so exquisitely gentle that her defences instantly crumbled. Slow and sweet, his mouth explored hers in a sensual tasting that evoked a desperate yearning inside her for him to hold her close and never let her go. He explored the shape of her mouth with his tongue, and there was no thought in her head to resist him when he probed between her lips in a caress that was so intensely erotic that she trembled with need.

And yet she recognised the restraint he had imposed on himself. She was clinging to him, pressing her slender curves eagerly against his rock-solid body, but for some reason he held back, dampening the passion between them to a slow burn rather than allowing it to blaze into a wild firestorm.

She realised that he was giving her a choice. He would not force her into his bed. But she was ashamed to admit that she wished he would sweep her into his arms and carry her into the bedroom. She did not want to think about the implications of having sex with him. She wanted him to seduce her and make love to her with all his considerable skill, so that conscious thought was obliterated and she could lose herself in the sensual mastery of his touch.

He traced his mouth over her cheeks, her eyelids, little teasing caresses that tormented her until with a soft moan she cupped his face with her hands and brought his mouth down on hers. Parting her lips beneath his, she initiated a bold exploration with her tongue.

Ramon's tenuous hold on his self-control shattered. 'Is this what you want, *querida*?' he growled, tightening his arms around her until she was welded to his hard frame and could be in no doubt of the urgency of his arousal, jabbing insistently between her thighs. She was his woman, and he kissed her with a fierce possessiveness, his hunger for her an unstoppable force that demanded appeasement.

Suddenly, explosively, the barriers shattered into pieces, releasing their mutual desire like molten lava flow from a volcanic heart. Lauren's lips were swollen when Ramon finally lifted his head and trailed burning kisses down her throat, over the smooth slopes of her upper breasts. Her nipples were tight and hot, tingling in anticipation of his touch, and she gave a shiver of pleasure when he drew the straps of her dress over her shoulders, lower and lower, until her breasts spilled into his hands.

'Your breasts were always incredibly sensitive,' he murmured hoarsely as he rolled her nipples between his fingers, squeezing and releasing until she made a keening sound in her throat. 'I have never wanted any woman the way I want you.'

The admission was torn from him as she tugged clumsily at his shirt buttons and ran her hands over his bare chest and abdomen, her fingers stilling when she reached the waistband of his trousers. His erection was so hard that Ramon feared he would come at any second, and with an impatient growl he reached around her, unzipped her dress, and tugged it down so that it pooled at her feet.

Tiny black lace knickers covered her femininity. He hooked his fingers in the elastic and deliberately held her gaze as he slowly drew them down her legs. 'You want me, Lauren,' he told her harshly, and to prove his point he slid his hand between her thighs and discovered the slick wetness of her arousal. 'You can't deny your need is as great as mine.'

Lauren could not deny it; she did not even attempt to try. She had missed him so much, ached for him for so many nights, that she simply did not possess the will-power to resist him. Everything seemed strangely distant—Matty, the knowledge that she could never mean anything to Ramon, her colleagues and bosses downstairs. Would it be so wrong to have this one night with him? her mind argued.

Recriminations could come later—but when Ramon dropped to his knees and parted her womanhood with gentle fingers, before closing his mouth around the sensitive nub of her clitoris, she curled her fingers in his hair and sobbed his name.

He explored her with his tongue, delving into her moist heat and stretching her a little wider with his finger to intensify her pleasure. 'Oh, now—please now.' Delicious little spasms were rippling through her, building quickly to a crescendo, but she wanted more.

'Tell me what you want, *querida*,' he demanded.

For a crazy second she wondered what he would say if she revealed that she wanted him to love her. But of course he never would, and at that moment nothing mattered but that he should possess her.

'I want you…inside me.' For a few tense seconds her confession simmered between them, and then with a muttered oath he swept her into his arms and strode into the bedroom. He dropped her onto the mattress and she watched, wide-eyed, as he stripped with violent haste, his boxers hitting the floor to reveal the powerful length of his arousal.

Lauren's mouth ran dry, but when he pulled her to the edge of the bed, spread her legs and stood between them, her faint wariness disappeared beneath a tidal wave of excitement and desire. He swiftly donned protection, and then with slow deliberation rubbed the tip of his penis up and down the silken folds of her opening. She gasped, and instinctively bent her knees to allow him to penetrate her, closing her eyes blissfully when he filled her with his thick, iron-hard shaft.

'I've missed you.' The stark admission caused her lashes to fly open, and as she met his gaze she glimpsed a fleeting emotion that disappeared before she could define it, leaving his expression once more unfathomable. She wanted to tell him that she had missed him too, that her very soul had felt empty without him, but her words were lost beneath the pressure of his mouth as he crushed her lips in a hungry kiss at the same time as he began to move within her.

She was so tight, Ramon thought as he sank deeper into her warm velvet embrace. And her eagerness suggested that she hadn't had sex very often during the past eighteen months. The thought filled him with a primitive satisfaction. It was time he reminded her just how good they were together. He thrust deeper and harder, setting a rhythm that soon elicited little whimpers of delight from her.

A coiling sensation was growing low in Lauren's pelvis, tightening with every powerful thrust as Ramon drove into her again and again. The sensations he was arousing were indescribable. Her entire body was thrumming with pleasure, and when he closed his mouth around first one nipple and then its twin, sucking hard on each rosy crest, she writhed beneath him.

She stared up at him—at the bunched muscles of powerful shoulders and the beads of sweat that glistened on his chest. His face was a taut mask and she sensed that he was close to the edge. A feeling of tenderness swept over her, and the need to satisfy the frantic demands of her own body became secondary to her yearning for him to experience the pleasure of sexual release.

He gripped her hips, and she tilted her pelvis so that he could drive even deeper into her, welcoming each devastating thrust and whispering a husky plea for him to take her faster, harder. With a groan he obeyed her, the last vestiges of his restraint decimated by her fiery passion. And suddenly Lauren found that she had reached the pinnacle. She had been so intent on giving him pleasure that she was unprepared when the coiling sensation deep inside her snapped, and spasm after spasm of exquisite sensation ripped through her.

Dear heaven, it had been so long since she had experienced such intense pleasure that she had forgotten the sheer wonder of climaxing in Ramon's arms. She squeezed her eyes shut to prevent her tears from escaping. Ramon must never know that, for her, making love with him was a beautiful and emotional experience. He did not *do* emotions—for him this was just sex, she accepted, as he gave one final savage thrust and groaned as his big body shook with the power of his release.

The silence in the room was broken by the sound of ragged breathing gradually slowing. Ramon felt strangely reluctant to disengage his body from Lauren's, but after a few minutes he rolled from her and saw that she was drifting off to sleep.

'You will be more comfortable under the covers,' he murmured, settling them both on the pillows and drawing the sheet over them.

'I must go back to my room,' Lauren muttered. 'I can't keep awake.'

The shock of Guy Hadlow's assault, followed by her utter capitulation to Ramon's hungry demands had left her exhausted, and a little voice in her head taunted that it was easier to allow sleep to claim her rather than face up to what she had done.

'I know!'

His gravelly laughter held a hint of something that sounded almost like tenderness. But she must have imagined it, Lauren told herself sleepily.

'Stay here with me,' he bade her firmly.

She was too weary to argue when he drew her into his arms so that her head rested on his chest. The rhythmic thud of his heart beneath her ear seemed to echo through her body, strong and steady, and she gave a sigh as her lashes drifted down.

Ramon smoothed her hair back from her face, switched off the bedside lamp, and could not hold back a satisfied smile in the darkness. Sex with Lauren was even better than he remembered. He hadn't felt this sated in a long time. The wine bar project would keep him in England for several weeks, and then, although it would be necessary for him to return to Spain, he would keep his London apartment and visit Lauren regularly.

His life had been mapped out from birth, and he accepted the obligations and responsibilities that came with being a *duque*. But before he settled down to a life of duty he deserved a final fling with this woman who could send his temperature soaring with one look from her cool grey eyes.

With that settled, Ramon fell asleep.

* * *

It was still dark when Lauren stirred, but she was instantly awake. Shame, guilt, and a whole host of other emotions were storming through her when she turned her head and saw Ramon sprawled on his back beside her. His face looked softer in sleep, and the thick black lashes fanning his cheeks were a piercingly sweet reminder of Mateo.

What a fool she had been—a weak-willed fool who had allowed the sweet pull of sexual desire to drown out the voice of caution in her head, she thought bitterly. She had spent the night in Ramon's bed, and now he would think she was willing to be his mistress again.

It would be impossible to keep Matty hidden from him, she realised, panic making her heart pound. She would have to leave PGH, leave London, take Matty away somewhere and pray that Ramon did not try to find her…

She took a shuddering breath. What on earth was she thinking? She could not uproot Matty from his home. She stared at Ramon's beautifully sculpted face. The shadow of dark stubble on his jaw gave him a strangely vulnerable air. He was not a demon, she reminded herself. He was the man she had fallen in love with—the man who had made love to her last night with tenderness as well as passion.

When she had ended their affair he had told

her he would not take her back, yet he had come to find her. Perhaps he had only come because of the fierce sexual chemistry between them, but what mattered was that he was here. She could no longer use the excuse that she did not know where to contact him. She was through with playing God. Ramon had a right to know that he had a son, and as soon as he woke she would tell him.

The sound of her mobile phone made her jump, and she quickly slid out of bed and hurried through to the sitting room, rifling through her handbag to answer it before it disturbed Ramon. She gave a faint smile when she saw that it was her mother calling. She'd warned Frances that Mateo invariably woke at dawn, and not to expect a lie-in.

'Mum?' She kept her voice low. 'Has Matty been awake for long?'

'Oh, Lauren…' Frances's voice shook. 'Lauren, Matty's not well.'

'What do you mean—he's not well?' An icy hand of fear gripped Lauren's heart. 'What's wrong with him?'

'He…he settled fine when I put him in his cot last night, and he slept well. But this morning I woke up when I heard him make a funny noise. It wasn't a cry…' Frances's voice wavered. 'More a sort of choking sound.'

Dear God! Lauren gripped her phone so hard that her knuckles whitened.

'Of course I rushed into his room,' her mother continued. 'And, well…he seemed to be having some kind of a fit. I called an ambulance immediately, and the medics are here now. They're going to take him to the hospital.'

'I'll go straight there,' Lauren told her mother urgently, and cut the call. Her dress and underwear were scattered on the carpet—a shameful reminder of how she had become a wanton creature in Ramon's arms last night. But at this moment she could think of nothing but being with her sick child.

Heart pounding with fear, she dragged the dress over her head and tore out of Ramon's suite, into the lift. Once back in her own room she changed into jeans and a jumper, snatched up her overnight bag, and minutes later was racing across the hotel's reception area. She did not allow herself to dwell on what might be wrong with Mateo. Her brain focused exclusively on the necessity to get to the hospital as quickly as possible. Nothing and no one else mattered right now—not even Ramon. She did not spare him a thought.

She cannoned into Alistair Gambrill, who was standing on the hotel steps, holding a set of golf clubs. 'Lauren, you're up early.' He frowned when he saw her tense expression. 'Is everything all right?'

'Matty's ill. I have to go,' she called over her shoulder as she flew down the steps. There was no time to stop and talk to the senior partner. Her baby was on his way to hospital, and the devil himself would not prevent her from being with him.

Ramon gunned his Porsche along the busy North London streets. It was late on Saturday afternoon, and there was a lot of traffic as he headed in the direction of Lauren's flat.

'Lauren left early this morning because her son is unwell.'

Alistair Gambrill's words played over and over in his head. *Her son!* Lauren had a child? *Dios!* His brain could not take it in. Whose child? He wanted, *demanded* an explanation, but all day her phone had been switched off, and his anger had increased with every abortive attempt to call her.

His mind re-ran the day, from the moment he had woken at the hotel and discovered that his bed was empty. At first he had thought she was in the bathroom, but when he had found that her clothes were gone he'd felt irritated that she must have returned to her room some time during the night. But he had reminded himself that Lauren had been upset by the idea that the other lawyers at PGH were discussing her relationship with him, and he understood her reluctance to risk being seen leaving his room.

With that in mind he had eaten breakfast in his suite and visited the hotel gym. He had only later learned from a casual remark by Alistair Gambrill of Lauren's early departure—and the astonishing reason for it.

'You'd never believe Matty was rushed into hospital this morning,' Lauren said for the umpteenth time, as she watched her son crawling energetically around the sitting room. 'He looks a hundred times better than he did when I saw him on the children's ward.'

'He looks a lot better than you,' her mother commented. 'You're still as white as a ghost.'

'I was worried.' Lauren grimaced at the understatement, and tears blurred her eyes. *Worried* came nowhere near the stark fear she had felt as she had raced to the hospital. The possibility that Mateo was seriously ill had filled her with terror, as well as guilt that she had left him with her mother while she had attended the Valentine's Ball. 'I shouldn't have gone to the wretched ball last night,' she said thickly.

'The doctor said that febrile convulsions are

fairly common in babies when they are running a high temperature,' Frances reminded her. 'He confirmed that Matty has a throat infection and that the antibiotics should take effect quickly. He's going to be fine, Lauren.'

'I know. I just keep thinking what if it had been worse? What if he'd had something life-threatening? I couldn't bear to lose him.' Lauren's voice wobbled and she lifted Mateo up and hugged him to her. 'I love him so much.'

Her legs suddenly felt weak, and she collapsed onto the sofa. She had been feeling unwell since they had brought Matty home from the hospital a few hours ago, but had put her pounding headache and aching limbs down to the after-effects of shock. Now she had developed a sore throat, and felt shivery. It seemed likely she had caught the virulent flu virus that had been going round the PGH offices recently. That was all she needed, she thought wearily.

The doorbell pealed. 'That's probably my taxi,' Frances murmured, getting to her feet. 'Are you sure you'll be all right if I go to Southampton tonight?'

'Of course I will,' Lauren assured her mother. 'You can't miss a world cruise—and you *must* go tonight if you're to board the ship at eight tomorrow morning.'

She rested her aching head against the back of the sofa, grateful that Matty was playing contentedly with a new toy for a few minutes. She could hear voices in the hall. Maybe her mother's taxi wasn't here yet, and a neighbour who had seen the ambulance arrive that morning had called to ask after the baby? Footsteps sounded in the hall. She glanced towards the living room door as it opened. Her mother walked in—and then Lauren gave an audible gasp at the sight of the dark and infinitely dangerous-looking man following closely behind Frances.

Ramon! A grim-faced Ramon, whose eyes were glittering with rage. Lauren instinctively tightened her grip on Mateo and swallowed when Ramon's gaze swung from her to her baby son.

CHAPTER FIVE

'LAUREN—Mr Velaquez has explained that he is one of your clients…' Frances's voice tailed to a halt as she glanced from her daughter to the darkly handsome man whom she had invited into the flat, and who was now staring grimly at Lauren and Mateo.

Silence fell in the room. A silence that simmered with an undercurrent of tension that made Lauren's skin prickle. She was barely aware of her mother. Her eyes were riveted on Ramon's face. He had paled beneath his tan, his shock palpable. She could not tear her gaze from him, and she watched as his shocked expression changed to one of bitter fury.

'So it's true—you have a child.' His voice was so harsh it was almost unrecognisable, his accent very pronounced. Silence stretched between them once more, shredding Lauren's nerves, before he spoke again. 'He is my son.'

It was a statement, not a question. The resem-

blance between Ramon and Matty was startling.
Lauren could not have denied the truth even if she
had wanted to, and she gave a tiny nod.

He swore violently, and Lauren flinched. 'You
kept my son a secret from me,' he said hoarsely,
disbelievingly. He stared at the baby and saw his
own features in miniature. There was no doubt
that Lauren was holding his child in her arms, but
his brain was struggling to comprehend what his
eyes were telling him.

And not just his eyes, he thought as he walked
jerkily across the room, moving without his usual
lithe grace. His heart, his soul recognised his own
flesh and blood. He did not understand how it had
happened, but that was immaterial now. Lauren
had given birth to his son—and had never told
him.

For the second time in his life Ramon tasted
the rancid bile of betrayal in his throat. The only
other occasion he had felt like this was when he
had been eighteen, standing in the doorway of a
hotel bedroom, fixated by the sight of the woman
he loved lying naked on the bed with another man.

'*Now* do you see why you cannot marry this
trollop?' his father asked from behind him.
'Catalina Cortez was never in love with you, my
son. It was all a trick, devised with her lover, to
seduce you into marriage so that she could claim

a vast divorce settlement. You have been taken for a fool, Ramon,' Estevan Velaquez had told him harshly. 'But fortunately no damage has been done—except to your pride, perhaps,' the *Duque* had added perceptively.

The disappointment in his father's eyes had intensified Ramon's humiliation, and as he had stared at Catalina he had vowed never to trust another woman again. Over the years that decision had served him well, for he had found most women to be untrustworthy. But Lauren had been different. One of the qualities he had most admired about her had been her honesty. He had spent his life surrounded by people who fawned on him and told him what they thought he wanted to hear, and he had found Lauren's tendency to speak her mind a refreshing change.

Now he knew that she no more deserved his trust than Catalina had, Ramon thought bitterly. Lauren had not cheated on him with another man, but she had cheated him out of the first months of his son's life, and he would never forgive her for her duplicity.

'How old is he?' he ground out, forcing the words past a peculiar constriction in his throat.

'Ten months.'

Lauren bit her lip. Ramon looked shell-shocked, almost haggard, and the terrible realisation was dawning inside her that she had been wrong to keep his son a secret from him. He was a playboy Spanish *duque*, who had freely admitted that he viewed marriage as an unwelcome duty necessary to begat the next Velaquez heir, she tried to reassure herself. But the look of *devastation* in his eyes tore at her conscience.

'Ten months?' he repeated harshly. 'You have kept my son from me for almost a year.' He did a quick mental calculation. 'You knew you were pregnant the night you ended our affair, didn't you? *Dios!*' He closed his eyes briefly, trying to take it in. '*Why*, Lauren?'

'Lauren—what's going on?' Frances interrupted in a shocked voice. 'Who is this man?' She stared warily at the formidable stranger dressed in black jeans, sweater and a leather jacket. 'Shall I call the police?'

'No. It's all right, Mum.' Lauren took a shaky breath. 'Ramon is Matty's father. I…I need to talk to him, and you need to go. I think your taxi is here now. Please don't worry,' she begged her mother, who looked as though she was going to argue. 'Everything is going to be fine.'

If only she could believe that, she thought a few minutes later, as she gave Frances a wave and shut the front door. Her headache had developed into an excruciating pain, as if someone was drilling through her skull. She longed to take some pain-killers and lie down on her bed for a few minutes, but instead she took a deep breath and walked back into the sitting room.

Ramon was standing by the mantelpiece, study-ing a photo of Mateo taken when he had been a few days old. He speared her with a savage glare. 'I don't even know his name,' he said, in a low tone that could not disguise his tightly leashed anger.

'It's Mateo.'

'Mateo.' Ramon spoke his son's name with a sense of wonder. His son—*his son*. He still couldn't take it in. Until now he had viewed fa-therhood simply as a duty he would have to fulfil at some point in the future. He had never actually envisaged what it would be like to have a child. But now he was faced with his son, whose features so resembled his own that it was like looking at a miniature version of himself, and he felt awed that this perfect, beautiful child was his.

Matty was sitting on Lauren's hip, his head resting on her shoulder, but he looked up enquir-ingly at the sound of his name and gave Ramon a gummy smile. The baby was usually wary of strangers, especially when he was tired, but to Lauren's shock he held his arms out to his father. Ramon moved closer, his hands visibly shaking as he touched his son for the first time, and Lauren felt a sudden, irrational feeling of panic. She did not want to let Matty go, but the baby smiled happily as Ramon lifted him and held him against his chest.

'Mateo.' Ramon stroked his son's silky black hair, and as he stared down into the baby's sherry-brown eyes that were the exact same shade as his own the tidal wave of emotion that swept through him threatened to unman him. He had missed most of the first year of his son's life. Lauren had stolen those irreplaceable months from him, and the knowledge filled him with black fury.

Lauren swallowed the tears that clogged her throat. Matty looked so small in Ramon's arms, and the look of tenderness in Ramon's eyes as he studied his son evoked a host of emotions in her. 'Matty is tired,' she said quietly. 'He usually has a nap about now. I'll put him in his cot.' She held out her hands to take the baby, but Ramon shook his head.

'I'll take him. Show me where he sleeps.'

It would be childish to refuse, and she could hardly snatch Matty out of Ramon's arms, she acknowledged as she reluctantly led the way down the hall to the tiny boxroom that served as a nursery.

'He's had a traumatic day,' Lauren explained a

few minutes later, after Ramon had carefully laid Mateo in his cot.

'Alistair Gambrill told me this morning that you had rushed home because your son was ill.'

So that was how he had found out about Matty. And now she could not deny Ramon the answers he clearly wanted. Her head felt as though it was about to split open, but she tried to ignore the pain and led the way back into the sitting room.

'What was wrong with Mateo?' Ramon demanded. 'He seems to be perfectly well now.'

'He had a fit this morning. My mother called an ambulance and he was rushed into hospital. Apparently it was what is called a febrile convulsion, brought on by a high temperature. Tests revealed that he has a throat infection, and the doctor prescribed a course of antibiotics. There should be no lasting damage, although babies who have had febrile convulsions are slightly more at risk of having them again,' she added shakily.

Tears filled her eyes once again, although she knew it was pathetic to cry when the doctor had assured her that Matty had been completely unharmed by the fit.

She dashed her hand across her face and glanced up, to find Ramon watching her through narrowed eyes. He had taken off his leather jacket, and suddenly he flung it forcefully onto a chair, his barely leashed violence making Lauren jump.

'Why did you do it, Lauren?' He caught hold of her shoulders in a bruising grip that made her cry out.

'Ramon! You're hurting me.'

'I could *kill* you,' he snarled. His face was a hard mask, his skin drawn taut over razor-sharp cheekbones. He glimpsed the fear in her eyes and felt infuriated that even in the midst of his anger Lauren's air of vulnerability got to him. He flung her from him, disgusted as much with himself as with her. 'You treacherous bitch. How could you deny me my own son?'

Lauren rubbed her shoulders and stared at him with huge, wary eyes. 'I didn't think you would want him.'

'You never gave me a choice.' Nostrils flaring, Ramon fought to control his temper. 'Why would you think that I would not want my own child?'

Lauren gave a bitter laugh. 'Because you told me that it was your duty to marry an aristocratic Spanish bride and provide a blue-blooded heir to continue the Velaquez line. I was going to tell you I was pregnant that last night, when we went to the Vine for dinner, but you made it clear that I meant nothing to you.'

She would never forget his appalled expression when she had given him an anniversary gift.

'You insisted that I could only ever be your mistress. I was afraid you would think that Matty wasn't a suitable heir—because I certainly don't have any noble ancestors,' Lauren continued in a low tone when Ramon gave her a scathing look. She bit her lip. 'From the moment I walked out of your apartment I was tormented by guilt and indecision. I didn't know what to do. I was torn between wanting to tell you that I was expecting your baby, and being afraid of your reaction. Many times—before Matty was born, and after—I brought up your number on my phone. But each time I lost my nerve and didn't put the call through,' she admitted huskily.

'I didn't want Matty to grow up feeling that he wasn't good enough to be part of the illustrious Velaquez family.' She voiced the fear that had gnawed at her. 'Children need to feel valued.' It was something she had learned when her father had left and she had realised how unimportant she was to him. 'Although you might have been willing to marry for duty, I wasn't.'

'You thought it better to bring Mateo up without a father?' Ramon accused her scathingly. 'What right did you have to deny him one of his parents? Did you ever think about what *he* might want?'

Lauren paled. She *had* felt guilty that Matty would grow up without a father, but it had seemed preferable to an uninterested father whom she had feared would regard fatherhood as an irksome duty.

'And how much more of his life were you going to steal from me?' Ramon demanded furiously. 'Would you *ever* have told me about him?' His blood ran cold. 'Or was that chance remark by Alistair Gambrill the only reason I discovered my child's existence?'

When she did not answer, he glared at her with bitter contempt.

'*Dios!* You slept with me last night, and even then you said nothing. What was all that about, anyway? Were you using me as a stud, in the hope of conceiving a sibling for Mateo?'

'*No!* Don't be ridiculous.' Lauren's temper flared at his outrageous accusation. 'You came on to *me*, if you remember. You danced with me all evening, and took me up to your room.'

'You came willingly enough.'

'Only because Guy had upset me. I never intended for things to turn out the way they did.' She looked away from him, colour flooding her cheeks—because she was lying, she admitted bleakly.

During the ball she had been intensely aware

of Ramon, and deep down she had longed for him to take her to his room and make love to her. Even now she was acutely conscious of him. Her traitorous body ached for him to touch her as he had touched her last night. The memory of how he had stroked his hands over her naked flesh and brought her to the peak of arousal with his clever fingers made her limbs tremble.

Ramon raked his hand through his hair and swung away from her, pacing around the small living room like an angry caged bear. 'Who cares for Mateo while you are at work all day? You told me your mother lives in Jersey, so presumably *she* is not involved in his upbringing?'

'He is in a daycare nursery. It's an excellent nursery—the absolute best,' she continued quickly, when Ramon frowned. The nursery fees were exorbitant, but she was happy to pay them for peace of mind that Matty was happy and well cared for.

'And when did you return to work?'

'When he was three months old.'

'*Dios mio!* You dumped him in daycare when he was just three months old?' There was genuine horror in Ramon's eyes. 'My sisters did not leave their babies' sides for the first years of their lives.'

Lauren gave him a startled look. 'I didn't even know you *had* sisters. In all the months that we were together you never spoke about your family.'

He shrugged. 'I learned long ago to guard my privacy, and that of my family, after a couple of ex-mistresses blabbed to the tabloids about my personal life. Even the colour scheme of my bathroom seems to be fascinating to some people,' he added dryly.

But there had been another reason why he had maintained a distance between himself and Lauren, Ramon admitted silently. Over the years he had learned to compartmentalise his life; in Spain he had been the son of a *duque*, who could never forget the life of duty that lay ahead of him, but in London he had enjoyed a playboy lifestyle. His relationship with Lauren had begun as just another affair with a pretty blonde, and because he had known that that was all it could ever be he had deliberately not allowed his two worlds to mix.

'You must have known that I wouldn't do something like that,' Lauren muttered, hurt by his lack of trust in her. It reinforced the fact that he had regarded her as just another casual lover, and once again she wondered how she had been stupid enough to believe he had started to care for her.

'Unlike your sisters, I live in the real world,' she said curtly. 'I had to go back to work to pay the bills. I'm not saying the situation is ideal, but I have done my very best for Matty. I even used to spend my lunch hour in the ladies' loo, expressing my breast milk so that the nursery staff could give it to him the next day.'

Her life in the first few months after she'd had Mateo had been a blur of exhaustion, worry, and guilty tears shed silently in the cloakroom at work in between meetings. Ramon would never understand what a terrible wrench she still found it to leave her baby for hours every day.

'It would have been better for him if you had held him in your arms and fed him yourself,' he said harshly. 'Breastfeeding is a crucial time, when the special bond between a mother and her child is formed.'

'I had no idea you were such an expert in childcare,' Lauren snapped, infuriated by his arrogance. 'I hate having to leave Matty, but I have no choice…'

'Yes, you do. You have always had a choice,' Ramon said bitterly. 'If you had told me you were expecting my child I would have ensured that you received the best care. My son would have been born in Spain and would have spent the past ten months at the Castillo del Toro, surrounded by his grandmother and his aunts and cousins—not here in this poky flat, farmed out to a nursery all day while you pursue your precious career.'

Poky flat…farmed out… Ramon's scathing indictment of the way she was bringing up Mateo rendered Lauren speechless with fury. But before she could formulate a reply he spoke again—this time in a cold, implacable voice that she found more frightening than his explosive temper.

'I want my son. And I will have him; do not doubt it, Lauren.'

The moment Ramon had laid eyes on his son he had realised he did not give a damn if the baby was not deemed to be of true Spanish noble blood because he had been born to an English mother. Mateo was his child, and he felt fiercely possessive and protective of him.

'It is obvious from Mateo's striking similarity to me that he is a Velaquez, but if you deny that I am his father I will demand a DNA test, and then I will take him to Spain, where he belongs.'

'You can't do that.' Lauren shook her head, and winced as starbursts of pain shot through her skull. She could not stop shivering, yet two minutes ago she had been burning up. Her legs must be trembling because she had a fever, but as she stared at Ramon's hard face fear swept through her, and she sank weakly onto the sofa. 'You have no right to take him,' she said shakily.

He slammed his hand down on the table, his temper exploding once again. 'Don't you *dare* talk to me about rights! What right did you have to keep my son from me? And what right did you have to deny Mateo his father? This is not about us,' Ramon said grimly. 'The only important thing is what is best for Mateo.'

'How can taking him away from me be best for him?' Lauren held her hand to her throbbing head and tried to think clearly. 'I may not have specialised in family law, but no court would separate a baby from his mother.'

'We'll see,' Ramon said coldly. 'I think it is entirely likely a judge would agree that it would be better for Mateo to live with his father, who is prepared to devote his life to him, within a huge extended family who will welcome him and love him, than with a mother who is at work all day while he is left in the care of nursery staff. A child of Mateo's age needs the security of being cared for mainly by one or two family members, and *I* will be there for him night and day.'

'Really?' Lauren said disbelievingly. 'What about when you are jet-setting around the globe for work? Or attending numerous social functions? I suppose you'll leave Matty with a nanny?'

'I intend to cut my business trips to a minimum, and to be frank I'm bored with parties. I would much rather spend my time with my son.'

He stared at Lauren's white face and hardened his heart against a faint flicker of sympathy. She had cold-bloodedly denied him his child, and she did not deserve his compassion.

'What you did was unforgivable,' he said harshly. 'You had better start praying you win that promotion Alistair Gambrill told me you are in line for, because you are going to need all the money you can get to pay for the custody battle—and for the appeal if I lose the first round, and then the next appeal. Do you get the picture, Lauren? I will never give up fighting for my son because I genuinely believe he will have a better life with me. Mateo is the Velaquez heir, and I don't understand how you could want to deny him his birthright.'

Lauren suddenly sneezed violently, and could not stifle a groan as pain tore through every muscle in her body. She still could not stop shivering, but when she pushed her hair back from her face her brow felt clammy with sweat. She rested her head against the back of the sofa, unaware of Ramon's sharp scrutiny.

He frowned when he saw that her skin was a strange grey colour. 'What's the matter with you?' he demanded tersely. 'You look terrible.'

She gave a mirthless smile. 'You don't think that might have something to do with the fact that you're threatening to take Matty from me?' Her throat felt as though she had swallowed shards of glass, and talking was agony. 'I must have picked up the flu virus that's been doing the rounds at work.' She dropped her gaze from the blazing fury in his. 'I'm sorry,' she whispered. 'I honestly believed you would want nothing to do with Matty—or, worse, consider him an obligation. But, whatever you think, I swear I have done my best to be a good mother to him.'

Dark eyes stared back at her, icy cold and unforgiving. 'Unfortunately I do not consider your best to be good enough.' He frowned when she sneezed again. '*Dios!* You are in no fit state to look after a baby. You can barely stand,' he growled as she got up from the sofa and swayed. 'I understand your mother is embarking on a cruise tomorrow and won't be around?'

Lauren gave a reluctant nod, and winced as the slight movement of her head sent more starbursts of pain through her skull.

Ramon pulled his phone from his pocket. 'I'll arrange for a private jet to collect us tonight. There is an airfield about twenty miles from here.'

'Collect us and take us where?' Lauren croaked, dismayed to find that she was losing her voice. She couldn't remember ever feeling so ill in her life, and the grim determination in Ramon's voice scared her to death.

'I'm taking my son to Spain—and you're coming

too. Unlike you, I believe that Mateo needs both his parents,' he said curtly.

'Oh, no.' She shook her head, and could not prevent a moan of agony. 'I won't let you take Matty anywhere,' she said wildly.

'Don't be ridiculous. You're ill, and he needs to be cared for until you are better. The only place he should be right now is with his family. My mother will be overjoyed to meet her new grandson, and I will hire a nurse who will watch over Mateo in case he should suffer more convulsions.'

A disgruntled wail sounded from along the hall. Matty often woke up grouchy after a late nap, and when Lauren hurried into his room he was standing up in his cot, rattling the bars and yelling so loudly that she felt her head would split open.

'Come on, sweetie, I expect you want your tea,' she murmured, trying to pacify him. But the baby was beside himself with temper, and wriggled so violently when she picked him up that she almost dropped him.

'Give him to me,' Ramon said grimly from the doorway. 'You don't have the strength to hold him.' He moved towards Lauren, his eyes focused on the hysterical baby.

His son had certainly inherited the Velaquez temper, he thought ruefully. Even at less than a year old it was clear that Mateo was a strong-willed little boy, who would need guidance from his father as well as his mother as he grew up.

'Mateo.' Ramon spoke gently yet firmly, and to Lauren's chagrin Matty stopped screaming and stared in fascination at the tall man who held out his hands. 'Come to your *papito, mi precioso.*'

Come to your daddy! Lauren caught her breath when Matty suddenly grinned and leaned towards Ramon. Every instinct inside her fought against the idea of handing her baby over, but Matty wanted to go, and she felt so weak that her knees sagged when Ramon took his son from her.

'Ramon…' she called him desperately.

He paused on his way out of the tiny nursery and flicked cold eyes over her. 'Get your coat,' he ordered harshly. 'The car will be here in five minutes.'

There was a picture of a cherub above her head. Lauren opened her eyes wider and saw that the cherub was part of an exquisite mural painted on the ceiling. She frowned, puzzling over how the mural had got there, and what had happened to her plain white bedroom ceiling.

'Ah, you're awake.'

The voice came from over by the window. Lauren squinted against the sunlight filtering through the blinds to see a pleasant-faced woman walking towards the bed.

'Hello, Lauren. I'm Cathy Morris,' the woman said gently. 'I'm an English nurse, and I've been helping Señor Velaquez to look after you.'

Ramon! Snatches of memory flooded Lauren's mind—blurred images of him carrying her up the steps of a plane. And then later she had opened her eyes briefly to find herself in a car, speeding towards a huge castle, ominous and forbidding in the moonlight, surrounded by jagged-edged mountains.

She struggled to sit up, shocked to discover that she had no strength. But Ramon had Matty. She had to get up and find him.

'I don't think you're ready to get out of bed just yet,' the nurse said, in a kind but firm tone. She eased Lauren back against the pillows and straightened the bedcovers. 'You've been very ill for the past four days, with a particularly nasty flu virus. Señor Velaquez has barely left your side. He has even been sleeping in the chair next to your bed so that he could see to you during the night. He's giving your son his breakfast at the moment, but I expect he'll be back here before long.'

When Cathy finally paused for breath Lauren mumbled weakly, 'So I'm in Spain? At Ramon's castle?'

'At the Castillo del Toro,' the nurse confirmed.
'It's a wonderful place—built in the thirteenth
century, apparently, and oozing with all the history of the Velaquez family. The English transla-
tion is the Castle of the Bull—named after one
Señor Velaquez's ancestors, who was renowned
for his fighting skills on the battlefield as well as
his prowess with the ladies.' Cathy grinned. 'I get
the impression from the local villagers that the
current *Duque* is as revered as his famous forefa-
ther.' She walked over to the door. 'I expect you'd
like a cup of tea—and then I'll help you into the
bathroom so that you can freshen up.'

In the nursery, along the hall from Lauren's room,
Ramon strapped his son into a highchair and surveyed the baby's immaculate clothes, scrubbed
face and shining, silky black curls with a sense of
achievement. Not that bathing and dressing Mateo
had been without its difficulties, he thought ruefully as he glanced down at his damp trousers
and shirt. He hadn't realised that a wet, wriggling
ten-month-old was as slippery as an eel, and after
towelling Mateo dry and struggling to fasten the
fiddly buttons of his romper suit Ramon felt he
deserved a medal.

'How did your *madre* do this every day before

going off to work?' he asked the baby, feeling a begrudging sense of admiration for Lauren.

His first four days of fatherhood had been an eye-opener, he admitted. Of course he could have simply handed Mateo over to the nurse, Cathy Morris, whom he had also employed as a nanny, but he was fascinated by this little human being who was his son, and he wanted to get to know him better.

All his life he had known that he had a duty to provide an heir and ensure the continuation of the Velaquez name, but he had never actually considered what it would be like to have a child, Ramon reflected. For one thing he had assumed that it would not happen for several years. He had accepted that he would eventually have to choose a suitable bride, but he had been in no hurry to sacrifice his freedom. Now the privilege of choice had been taken from him. He had a child, and he would never be free again. But as he stared into Mateo's sherry-brown eyes it struck him that his freedom to jet off around the world whenever he felt like it was a small price to pay for his son.

'Breakfast time,' he announced to Mateo, when a maid entered the nursery bearing a tray.

He picked up the bowl of milky cereal, filled a spoon, and offered it to the baby—who stubbornly refused to open his mouth.

'Come on, *chiquito*, it's good,' Ramon said persuasively. 'Try it for *Papà*, hmm?' Instead, Mateo tried to grab the spoon. 'Okay, you want to be independent and feed yourself?'

Maybe his son was a child genius? he mused as he handed the baby the spoon and set the bowl down on the highchair's tray.

'You do it, then. No, Mateo—with the spoon…' In disbelief Ramon watched Mateo pick up the bowl and upend its contents on top of his head, completely covering his mop of curls.

'Now I'll have to bath you all over again!' Ramon raked his hand through his hair.

He stared at Mateo, and the baby stared solemnly back at him, his rosebud mouth suddenly curving into an angelic smile. And in that moment Ramon fell utterly and irrevocably in love.

He threw back his head and laughed until he ached. 'You're a monster—you know that?' He lifted Mateo out of the highchair, his laughter dying as he hugged the baby to him. 'You are my son, and I will never be apart from you again,' he vowed fiercely.

A faint sound made him swing round, and he stiffened when he saw Lauren standing in the doorway. She looked pale and fragile, but it was the gleam of tears in her eyes that caused Ramon to frown.

'Why are you out of bed?' he demanded roughly. 'Cathy told me you were awake, but not strong enough to get up yet.'

Lauren swallowed, unable to tear her eyes from the sight of her son sitting contentedly in his father's arms. 'I wanted to find Matty,' she said huskily. 'The nurse said that you were giving him his breakfast.' She could not disguise her surprise that Ramon had wanted to take care of the baby rather than allow the nanny to see to him. He even looked different, she noticed. In faded jeans and a black polo shirt, rather than one of the designer suits that she was used to seeing him wear, he looked relaxed and somehow more human than the coldly arrogant, aristocratic *duque* who had stormed into her flat and threatened to fight her for their child.

Ramon glanced at the cereal plastering Matty's hair and gave a rueful grimace. 'As you can see, giving him his breakfast has not been a resounding success.'

Lauren gave him a faint smile. 'I can't count the number of times he has done that at home—usually on a morning when I've been running late for work. But he doesn't like to be fed. Even at this age he's very determined and wants to do everything for himself.'

'Rather like his mother,' Ramon commented

dryly. 'It can't have been easy, caring for him on your own and holding down your job, but you never considered asking for my help—did you, Lauren?'

She heard the latent anger in his voice and bit her lip. 'I didn't know how you would feel about having a baby,' she mumbled.

Ramon made an impatient sound. 'It's a pity you didn't ask me.'

Guilt surged through Lauren once more. She could stand here all day, trying to defend her actions, but in her heart she accepted that she had been wrong not to tell Ramon he had a son. She could not look at him, and instead glanced around the nursery. Through a half open door she could see an *en suite* bathroom. 'I'll run Matty another bath,' she said hurriedly, desperate to escape Ramon's accusing gaze.

Matty loved bath-time, and was perfectly happy to spend another twenty minutes playing in the bubbles.

'He's a real water baby,' Ramon said, smiling at Matty's squawk of displeasure when at last he lifted him out of the water and Lauren wrapped the disgruntled baby in a fluffy towel. 'In a month or so, when the weather is warmer, I'll take him in the pool. It will be good for him to learn to swim at an early age.'

His words made Lauren's heart jolt. She could not stay in Spain for *months*. She needed to get back to work. The mortgage on her flat would not pay itself. But she certainly did not intend to leave Matty here at the Castillo del Toro.

She followed Ramon back into the nursery, and her heart clenched when she watched him tenderly drying Matty. For such a big man he was amazingly gentle. Tears blurred her eyes. If only she had known this side of Ramon perhaps she would have acted differently. But when he had spoken of his duty to father an heir she had assumed from his tone that he did not relish the prospect of having a child. Clearly she had been wrong. She could see that already there was a special bond between father and son, and innate honesty forced her to acknowledge that she had no right to try and break it.

Ramon glanced at her white face and frowned. 'You look terrible. Go back to bed. I'll dress Mateo and take him downstairs to my mother,' he continued when Lauren shook her head. 'Go,' he insisted. You do not need to be here. I can take care of him fine without you.'

The words felt like a knife through her heart, and with a low cry she hurried out of the nursery, wondering despairingly what on earth she was going to do.

CHAPTER SIX

A FEW minutes after Lauren had returned to her room a maid arrived, with a pot of tea and a couple of freshly baked rolls that smelled temptingly good. She couldn't remember the last time she had eaten, although she had a vague memory of sipping water from a glass on several occasions while a strong arm supported her head and shoulders.

Had that been Ramon—who, according to the nurse, had spent the last four nights in the chair close to her bed? She frowned when she glanced down at the nightgown she was wearing, and it struck her that someone must have removed her jeans, sweatshirt and underwear. It must have been Cathy, she assured herself, her cheeks growing hot at the idea that Ramon might have undressed her.

She drank two cups of tea and managed half a roll before crossing the room to the *en suite* bathroom. The sight of her reflection in the mirror was a shock. She couldn't do much about her hollow cheeks and pale complexion, but at least she could be clean. Stripping off her nightdress, she quickly stepped into the shower, relishing the feel of the spray cleansing her body and the lemony scent of the shampoo that she worked into her hair.

'What the *hell* are you doing?'

The sound of a familiar gravelly voice coincided with Ramon's sudden appearance as he opened the door of the shower cubicle and stood glaring at her. Face flaming, Lauren realised that she would have to reach past him to grab a towel. Instead she frantically tried to cover certain pertinent areas of her body with her hands.

'I could ask you the same question,' she snapped.

'It's a bit late for modesty now, when I have spent the past few nights sponging your body to try and bring down your fever,' he said grimly. 'But at least you've finally got some colour in your cheeks.' He took pity on her and threw her a towel. 'As to what I'm doing here—I came to check that you had gone back to bed. I might have known you would be stupid enough to try and shower without assistance.'

'I am not stupid.' Lauren gave him a furious look. 'I'm feeling much better, and I don't need help.' She refused to admit that her legs felt dangerously unsteady, but of course they chose that minute to give way, so that she would have collapsed onto the floor of the shower if Ramon had not caught her.

'Of course you don't,' he said sardonically as he swept her into his arms and strode into the bedroom. 'But it's one thing to cause harm to yourself with your obsessive independence, and quite another when it affects our son.'

'I never did anything to harm Matty,' she said sharply. 'The day nursery he attends is excellent— the staff adore him, and he seems quite happy there.' It was she who was miserable when she left her baby each morning, and she frequently spent the train journey to work trying to hold back her tears.

She clutched the towel to her when Ramon set her on her feet. He pulled open a drawer in the bedside cabinet and handed her a gossamer-fine peach silk nightgown that definitely did not belong to her.

'You were so ill when we left your flat that I had to carry you down to the car, and I forgot to pack you any clothes,' he told her. 'I've ordered new things for Mateo, and a few items for you, but you'll have to shop for more when you are feeling better.'

'That won't be necessary,' Lauren said tensely. 'Matty and I won't be staying long. You can't *make* us stay here,' she cried, when Ramon's face hardened.

'I intend to do what is best for my son,' he said ominously. 'Why do you want to uproot him from his home, separate him not just from me but from his grandmother and the extended family he has already bonded with?'

'His home is in England,' Lauren choked.

'But regrettably most of his waking hours are spent in daycare.'

Ramon strolled over to the window, and while his back was turned Lauren hurriedly donned the nightgown, dismayed to find that her hands were trembling. There was a comb on the dressing table and she tugged it through her hair's wet tangles before blasting it with a hairdryer.

She jumped when Ramon came up behind her, took the dryer and began to run his fingers through her hair to aid the drying process. It was soothing, and evocatively intimate, and she had to fight the urge to close her eyes and lean back against him.

'Does it have to be a battle?' she pleaded. 'We both want to do the best thing for Matty. Can't we come to an amicable agreement on how we should care for him?'

His eyes met hers in the mirror. 'I think that is possible—as long as we both put Mateo's needs first.' He swung her into his arms before she had time to protest, and carried her back over to the bed. 'You need to rest. You've been very ill, and it will be a few days yet before you fully regain your strength.'

'I want to be with Matty,' Lauren argued. 'Who is looking after him?'

'My mother has taken him for a walk in the gardens.' Ramon glanced at his watch. 'If he follows the pattern of the last few days he will fall asleep, and then my dear *madre* will watch over him like a hawk until he wakes. She is utterly smitten with her new grandson,' he added dryly.

It was ridiculous to feel jealous of this new woman in Matty's life, Lauren told herself, but her eyes blurred with tears all the same. 'I miss him,' she said thickly.

'He's missed you too. The only way we could settle him at night was to lie him beside you in your bed. Once he was asleep I carried him to the nursery.'

Ramon's jaw tightened. If he had needed proof that his baby son needed his mother, the sight of Mateo curled up against Lauren while his sobs gradually subsided had surely been it. The close bond between mother and son was undeniable— but Mateo needed his father too, and to Ramon's mind there was only one logical solution that would allow his baby to be brought up by both his parents.

'I'll bring Mateo up to see you after his nap.'

He paused and studied Lauren, his eyes drawn to the rounded contours of her breasts and the slightly darker skin of her nipples, visible through the sheer fabric of the nightgown. She had run such a high fever while she had been ill that it had been necessary for him to strip her and sponge her naked body on several occasions. He had done so with clinical efficiency, his libido kept firmly under control. But now she was awake, watching him with her cool grey eyes, he was unbearably tempted to join her on the bed, peel the wisp of peach silk from those creamy breasts and take each rosy nipple in his mouth.

How could he still desire her when she had callously deprived him of his son for almost a year? he asked himself angrily, swinging away to stand by the window in the hope that she would not notice his powerful arousal. When he had first discovered that she had kept Mateo from him he had hated her, but during the days and nights that he had nursed her through her illness his anger had cooled, and he had forced himself to consider his own behaviour.

Lauren had accused him of being a playboy who had only wanted her for sex, and he could not deny the truth of that accusation. During their affair he had never considered a long-term relationship with her. His future had been mapped out: marriage—eventually—to a Spanish woman from his own elite social circle, who would provide him with the next Velaquez heir.

And yet, although he had refused to admit it, Lauren had got to him in a way that none of his numerous previous mistresses ever had.

'Who is Donny?' he asked her abruptly.

Lauren gave him a startled glance. 'He's my father,' she said after a moment. 'His name is Donald. When I was a child I used to call him Donny, instead of Dad, and his pet name for me was Laurie. It was just a silly thing between us.' She hesitated. 'Why do you ask?'

'You kept muttering his name when you were ill.'

Lauren had a vague memory of dreaming about her father. He had been walking down the garden path, holding a suitcase. It had been a dream re-enactment of the day that Donald Maitland had walked out on his wife and daughter. She had been crying and tugging on his sleeve, begging him not to leave her. She prayed she hadn't wept in her sleep. It was embarrassing to think that Ramon might have seen her crying. Impossible to glean anything from his shuttered expression.

So Donny wasn't her lover. But that wasn't to say that Lauren did not have a lover back in

England, Ramon brooded. The idea of some unknown man staying at her flat, possibly taking on
the role of stepfather to Mateo, made him want to
smash his fist into the wall.

'When you found out that you were pregnant
you *should* have told me—for Mateo's sake,' he
said harshly, unable to control his anger. 'It would
have been far better for him if you had given up
your job and been a full time mother. I would have
looked after both of you…'

'I didn't want your money,' Lauren said sharply.

'Perhaps you didn't, but it would have been in
Mateo's best interests if you had involved me,'
he said inexorably. 'Because of your selfishness
Mateo was denied his father for the first months
of his life, and he has spent far too much time in
the care of nursery staff when he could have been
here with his family.'

Her selfishness! Lauren was struck dumb by
Ramon's accusation. She had been self*less*. She
had devoted her life to Matty. Did Ramon think
she *enjoyed* leaving her baby every day?

But her conscience prickled with the knowledge
that there were some grains of truth in what he
had said. Ideally she would have liked to have
been with Matty constantly for his first year, but
one of the reasons she had not told Ramon he had
a son was because of her stubborn pride. He had

made it clear that she meant nothing to him, and so she had doggedly chosen to bring Matty up on her own—even though that had meant returning to work when he was only a few months old.

The guilt that had so often racked her when she dropped Mateo at the nursery churned in her stomach now. Ramon had scathingly told her that doing her best for Matty had not been good enough, and although she hated to admit it maybe he had a point?

She suddenly felt desperately tired. A legacy of the flu, she supposed. Tears filled her eyes, and she blinked frantically to dispel them. Dealing with Ramon was emotionally draining at the best of times, and they still had to discuss arrangements for sharing custody of their son.

'I have only ever wanted to do the right thing for Matty,' she told him thickly.

Ramon moved closer to the bed, and stared down at her with a hard gleam in his eyes that filled Lauren with a sudden sense of foreboding. 'In that case,' he said coolly, 'I assume you have no objection to marrying me?'

'I assume you're joking?' Lauren retorted after a lengthy stunned silence. Anger gripped her. 'You don't want to marry me, so don't try to pretend you do. I didn't even make it to girlfriend status when we were together. You only ever saw me as your mistress, and the fact that I have given birth to your child is not a good enough reason to tie us down in a relationship neither of us wants. We can both be involved in Matty's upbringing without some farcical marriage,' she insisted desperately when Ramon said nothing and simply surveyed her with his dark, unfathomable gaze.

'How?' he demanded bluntly.

'Well…' Lauren struggled to envisage how it would actually be possible for them both to care for Mateo when they lived in different countries. 'Maybe you could buy a house in England and he could stay with you when you visit,' she suggested, instantly disliking the idea that she might have to spend days, even weeks apart from Matty while he was with his father.

'I have already made it clear that Mateo will live permanently at the Castillo del Toro.'

'But it would be difficult for me to move to Spain and find a job. I speak Spanish reasonably well, but I am not familiar with the legal system over here. I would probably have to study for a Spanish law degree.'

Ramon shrugged, indicating his indifference to her concerns about her career. 'As my wife you will not need to work. I will provide you with everything you could possibly need.'

'I don't *want* you to keep me,' Lauren argued,

panic surging up inside her. 'I've worked hard to have a good career, and I value my independence.' The idea of being reliant on Ramon for money and a home filled her with horror. She had first-hand experience of how those things could be snatched away.

He stared at her speculatively. 'What do you value most, Lauren? Your independence, or your son? Because you cannot have both,' he told her, in an implacable tone that made her heart plummet.

'This is ridiculous,' she said shakily, her hand trembling as she pushed her hair back from her face. 'You can't want to marry me. I'm not a blue-blooded Spanish woman, and I wouldn't know how to be a *duquesa*.'

'It's true you are not an ideal choice,' Ramon told her with brutal frankness. 'But you are the mother of my son, and for his sake I have a duty to marry you so that he can grow up in the care of both his parents.'

Lauren felt as though prison bars were closing around her, trapping her. In desperation she tried another approach. 'You must see that it would never work. For a start, how would you feel to be married to a woman you don't love?'

'Love was never on my agenda,' he said dismissively. 'I do not consider it a prerequisite for a successful marriage. We both want to be with our son while he grows up, and I believe we are adult enough to be able to work things out. We were friends once,' he reminded her. 'And we proved on the night of the Valentine's Ball that we are still sexually compatible—wouldn't you agree, *querida*?' he demanded, his voice suddenly so toe-curlingly sexy that Lauren felt a tightening sensation deep in her pelvis.

She snatched a breath when he dropped down onto the edge of the bed and slowly ran his finger down the valley between her breasts. She was instantly agonisingly aware of him—of the distinctive scent of the cologne he always wore, the way his black hair gleamed like silk in the sunlight, and the sensual curve of his mouth that was so tantalisingly close to her own.

Pride belatedly came to her rescue, and she angrily pushed his hand away. 'That night was a mistake, and I regret that it ever happened,' she said shakily.

'Really?' he drawled sardonically.

Following his gaze, Lauren saw that her nipples were jutting provocatively against the sheer silk nightdress. Blushing furiously, she yanked the sheet up to her neck. She still felt horribly weak from her illness, and she wouldn't be surprised if Ramon had been relying on that to bulldoze her into doing what he wanted. But she wasn't an immature girl, in awe of him, she was a confident career woman and it was vital she took control of the situation.

'I won't allow you to intimidate me,' she told him fiercely, 'and I am certainly not going to marry you.'

'Then I hope you are prepared for a custody battle.'

Taking her by surprise, Ramon stood up and strode across the room. He glanced back at her from the doorway.

'And I hope you are prepared to lose—because I will never give up my son,' he said grimly, leaving her staring after him, her heart pounding with fear.

After Ramon had gone Lauren leapt out of bed— and then had to steady herself for a few moments as her head swam. The weakness in her limbs was infuriating, and made her realise how unwell she must have been. She had to get Matty away from the castle, she thought frantically. It would be necessary to borrow some of the clothes Ramon had bought her, but she would return them to him the minute she got back to England.

The dresses hanging in the wardrobe were exquisite creations, from a top design house. Lauren made a quick search for her jeans and sweatshirt, feeling reluctant to wear any of the clothes Ramon had provided, but there was no sign of any of her belongings. At last she chose a simple wrap-dress in dove-grey silk, and kitten heel shoes in a matching shade. A drawer in the dresser revealed several sets of beautiful underwear. She had a weakness for pretty knickers and bras, and she slipped them on with guilty pleasure, assuring herself that she would send Ramon a cheque to cover their cost.

Her plan was to find Matty and then call a taxi to take them to the airport. She was sure Ramon would assume that she was resting in her room, and with luck she could escape from the castle before he realised she had gone. But when she stepped out into the long corridor she had no idea which way to go. To her relief, a maid appeared around a corner.

'Where is Señor Velaquez?' she asked the young woman, thankful that she spoke Spanish reasonably well. She had picked it up as a child, when her parents had taken her on holiday to Spain every summer, and she had opted to study Spanish rather than French at school.

She had a sudden flashback to her first dinner-date with Ramon, when she had surprised him by speaking to him in his own language. Sherry-brown eyes gleaming wickedly, he had proceeded to teach her several Spanish words and phrases that had definitely *not* been part of the school curriculum. The sexual chemistry between them had sizzled, and when he had suggested going back to his apartment for a drink she had willingly agreed, knowing that he would make love to her, and impatient to experience the passion his sensual smile promised.

They had shared so many good times during their affair, she thought, her heart aching as memories flooded her mind. It hadn't just been the amazing sex; they had talked and laughed, visited art galleries, and walked for miles around the London parks. He had made love to her under a weeping willow tree in the middle of a heavy rain shower, and once they had got so carried away while out in a rowing boat on the Serpentine in Hyde Park that they had nearly capsized.

Her steps slowed. Ramon had said he believed they were adult enough to work things out for the sake of their child—but how could she possibly marry him knowing that he would never love her? It was a pathway to certain heartbreak, but so too was a legal battle over Matty—a battle she was not at all sure she would win, she thought bleakly.

'I want to find my son,' she told the maid urgently. 'Do you know where he is?'

'*Sí.*' The maid nodded. 'Follow me and I will take you to him.'

Under different circumstances Lauren would have liked to linger and study the dozens of rooms the maid took her past—rooms with stunning murals on the ceilings and exquisite tapestries on the walls, filled with beautiful antique furniture and even ancient suits of armour. And yet, despite being stuffed with historical artefacts, many of which were undoubtedly very valuable, the castle still felt like a home rather than a museum.

This was Matty's heritage, she thought as she followed the maid down a magnificent sweeping staircase and across a vast oak-panelled hall hung with portraits of dark, proud looking men whom she guessed were Ramon's ancestors. The castle and its ancient history were her son's birthright.

At the far end of the hall stood a set of doors, one of which was slightly ajar, revealing a modern addition to the castle: a beautiful glass conservatory that overlooked the extensive gardens beyond. Sunshine streamed through the windows onto the women and children who were sitting on the sofas or, in the children's case, sprawled on the floor around a laughing baby boy.

Mateo seemed completely at home amongst all these strangers, Lauren thought bleakly. She guessed that the older, rather regal-looking woman was Ramon's mother, and the three younger

women—one of whom was heavily pregnant—
must be his sisters.

She stood behind the half-open door and watched
Matty. He was sitting on a rug, surrounded by a
group of little girls and boys. The children were
teaching him to clap his hands, laughing and chat-
tering in Spanish, and to Lauren's amazement
Matty already seemed to understand them and
was grinning happily.

He belonged here. The thought struck her like
an arrow through her heart. With his jet black
curls and light olive skin he was the image of his
cousins, but he shared more than a physical re-
semblance with them. Matty was a Velaquez—a
member of the Spanish nobility. This castle was
his rightful home, and these people were his
family. How could she take him away, back to
her undeniably small flat, to a lifestyle that was
far from ideal? She hated leaving him at the nursery all day, but she had believed that she had no
choice.

Her choices now were not great, she thought
dismally. She could agree to a loveless marriage,
give up her job and her independence, and be tolerated here at the castle for no reason other than
that she was Matty's mother. Or she could risk a
court battle with Ramon, the outcome of which
would at best only give her shared custody of her

son, and might conceivably result in Ramon being allowed to keep Matty in Spain while she was awarded the right to visit him only a few times a year.

There was no choice, she acknowledged dully. She would rather die than be separated from her baby.

Five minutes later Ramon found her in the great hall, standing as cold and white as if she had been carved from marble as she watched Mateo and his cousins in the conservatory beyond.

'You look like death,' he said sharply when he came up to her. 'You shouldn't have come down-stairs.'

At last she turned her head to him, and the glis-ten of tears clinging to her lashes evoked a curious pain in his gut. 'Lauren…?'

'You win,' she said, in a voice as brittle as glass. 'I can't take Matty away from here—from his family. But I can't live without him.' She swal-lowed and then went on quickly, before her cour-age deserted her, 'And so, for him, I'll marry you.'

She made it sound as though she was offering herself as a human sacrifice, Ramon thought ir-ritably. *Dios*, he was a billionaire *duque*, and from now on she would live a life of luxury. 'Had you considered that marriage to me might not be the ordeal you seem to think it will?' he asked curtly. 'As my wife, you will want for nothing.'

'How do you know what I want?' Lauren said quietly. His words tore at her heart, for she would always long for the one thing he could never give her.

Muttering an imprecation, Ramon steered her into his study, strode over to his desk and took something from a drawer. 'Now that we are formally engaged you will wear this,' he told her, opening a velvet box to reveal a ring that drew a gasp from Lauren.

It was plainly an antique—an enormous ruby surrounded by a circle of diamonds and another circle of smaller rubies.

'It's a monstrosity,' she muttered, voicing the first thought that entered her head as Ramon took her cold hand and slid the ring onto her finger. It was a fraction tight over her knuckle, and felt heavy and cumbersome.

'Only *you* could describe a ring that was recently valued at a million pounds as a monstrosity,' Ramon said dryly. 'For countless generations every Velaquez bride has worn this ring, and my family will expect you to continue the tradition.'

A million pounds! 'But suppose I lose it?' Lauren argued as she stared at the huge ring in horror. 'Ramon, surely there's no need? It's not as if we are marrying for conventional reasons. We're not in *love* with each other,' she explained sharply when his dark brows rose quizzically.

'I doubt that love was a factor in many of my ancestors' choices of brides,' he replied laconically. 'For most marriage was a business arrangement, between high-born families.'

While Lauren brooded on his words he gripped her elbow and led her back out of his study and across the hall, to the doors leading to the conservatory.

'My mother, however, is under the illusion that ours is a love-match,' he told her grimly, 'and I have no intention of shattering her romantic ideals.'

'Meaning what, exactly?'

Sherry-brown eyes clashed with stormy grey ones. 'Meaning that in front of my family you will act the part of my love-struck fiancée.'

'Sorry, but I'm not that good an actress,' Lauren muttered sarcastically.

'Perhaps this will help you get into character.'

Ramon's dark head swooped before she realised his intention, and her startled gasp was lost beneath the hungry pressure of his mouth. She was unprepared for the thrust of his tongue between her lips, and to her shame white-hot, rampant desire swept through her as he explored her with a bold eroticism that left her weak and trembling and clinging to him for support.

She was scarlet-cheeked when Ramon finally broke the kiss, and her embarrassment intensified when she discovered that he had opened the door while he had been kissing her and they were in full view of everyone in the conservatory.

'Well, Ramon, I hope you are about to announce your engagement and spare all our blushes,' commented one of the young women in an amused voice.

'I am,' Ramon replied, triumph in his voice as he slid his arm around Lauren's waist and drew her forward. He led her over to the older woman, who stood up from the sofa as they approached. '*Madre*, this is Lauren—the mother of my son and, I am happy to say, soon to be my wife.'

His gentle, *loving* tone caused Lauren's steps to falter. It was pathetic to wish that his tender smile was genuine, she told herself angrily. He was only turning on the charm in front of his family. But she could not drag her eyes from his face, and her heart hammered beneath her ribs when he dropped a butterfly-soft kiss on her lips.

'Lauren—welcome.' Ramon's mother spoke in English, and to Lauren's surprise took her hands and kissed her on both cheeks. 'I am Marisol, and these are my daughters: Alissa, Juanita and

Valentina—who you might have guessed is expecting twins.'

Marisol Velaquez was tall and elegant, her beauty in no way diminished by the fact that her hair was now pure silver rather than the jet-black of her children and grandchildren. Lauren liked her instantly, and her fear that Ramon's mother would not approve of him marrying an English woman rather than a member of the Spanish nobility was allayed by the warmth of the older woman's smile.

'We are delighted to meet you, Lauren, and so sorry that you have been ill.' Ramon's sister Juanita, who had first spoken, now addressed Lauren in perfect English. 'Ramon explained that you had a high fever. It is fortunate that Mateo did not contract the virus.' She glanced down at two of the children, who were tickling Matty, making him squeal with laughter. 'As you can see,' she said with a smile, 'his cousins adore him already.'

Lauren was in no doubt that Ramon's family had taken her son into their hearts—especially his grandmother, she thought heavily, when she noted the soft expression on Marisol Velaquez's face. She knelt down in front of Matty, her heart aching with love for him. He immediately held out his arms and she hugged him to her, closing her eyes as she breathed in the delicious scent of her baby. He was her *life*, and she would do anything to be with him—even marry a man who had arrogantly stated that he did not consider love to be a prerequisite for marriage.

It took every ounce of her energy to stand up with Matty in her arms. She was sure he had grown during the past four days when she had been ill. He was certainly heavier, she thought wryly—or perhaps he only felt so because the flu had left her horribly weak.

'Allow me to take him,' Ramon's mother said gently. 'You are not strong enough yet to hold this fine big baby.'

Silly tears blurred Lauren's eyes as she handed Matty over to his grandmother. But Marisol was right. Her arms were already aching from the effort of holding him. So much for her earlier plan to snatch him and take him from the castle, she thought miserably.

'Come—it's time you were back in bed,' Ramon told her, sweeping her into his arms and ignoring her protest. 'The sooner you are fully recovered, the sooner I can make you my wife,' he added, with a mocking gleam in his eyes that made Lauren itch to slap him.

'I can walk,' she told him furiously as he strode out of the conservatory and across the hall. 'Your family can't see us now, and there's no need to act the part of loving fiancé on my account. Unlike your mother, I'm under no illusions about you.'

'Perhaps not,' he said evenly, 'but you've had the good sense to agree to marry me to keep your son, and for Mateo's sake it will be better if we end hostilities and try to be friends.'

Lauren seethed silently while he carried her up the stairs and along various corridors until they reached her room. 'How can you expect friendship from me when you have blackmailed me into marriage?' she demanded bitterly when he set her on her feet. 'You have callously used my love for Matty to get your own way.'

'I have done what is best for our son,' he countered inexorably. 'Mateo needs both of us.'

Before Lauren had time to react, he spun her round and unzipped her dress.

'What do you think you're doing?' She tried to bat his hands away but he ignored her and tugged the dress over her hips so that it slithered to the floor.

'You look even better in that underwear than I visualised when I chose it,' he drawled, the sudden heat in his gaze scorching her skin as he turned her back to face him and rested his eyes deliberately on her breasts.

To Lauren's shame her nipples instantly hardened and strained against the sheer lace bra cups, and she closed her eyes to shut out his mocking smile. 'The wedding will be *very* soon, *querida*,' he murmured. 'The best place for you to recuperate from your illness is in my bed.'

He only had to look at her and she was on fire for him, she thought despairingly. Her breasts felt heavy, and a tremor ran through her when he placed his hands on either side of her waist. She lifted her head blindly, thinking that he was going to kiss her, but her eyes flew open in shock when he drew back the covers and pushed her gently into bed.

'I'm glad you share my impatience,' he said in an amused voice, 'but you are not nearly strong enough yet for what I have in mind.'

'I hate you,' Lauren muttered grittily, burning up with mortification. She jerked her head to one side when he leaned over her, but he gripped her chin and forced her to look at him as he swooped and captured her mouth in a punishing kiss intent on proving his mastery.

She should resist him. Her brain knew it, but unfortunately her body did not agree. Molten heat coursed through her veins, and her limbs shook with need as he lowered his body onto hers. His tongue probed the tight line of her lips until with a moan she parted them so that he could delve into her moist warmth. She did not *want* to want him, and bitterly resented his power over her, but like it or not she was racked with hot, urgent desire, and with a low moan she cupped his face and kissed him with a fierce passion that she could not deny.

'I love the way you hate, *querida*,' Ramon drawled when he finally broke the kiss and they both dragged oxygen into their lungs. He got up from the bed and watched dispassionately as she dragged the sheet over her half-naked body. 'Blackmail is an ugly word. I may have coerced you into marrying me, for our son's sake, but however much I desire you I would never force you to share my bed. Fortunately I won't have to—will I, Lauren?'

She gave him a furious glare. 'Don't sulk,' he chided. 'Passion is as good a basis for marriage as any other—particularly when combined with our mutual desire to do the best for Mateo. What else is there to wish for?'

Love! Lauren wanted to cry. She wanted him to love her as she had loved him practically since the day she met him. But at this particular moment she felt so angry with him for demonstrating his power over her that she longed to throw a heavy object at his head.

'Get out,' she snapped, goaded beyond bearing by his arrogant smile.

'That's no way to talk to the man you are soon going to promise to honour with your body.'

Ramon wondered if Lauren had any idea how tempted he was to strip out of his clothes and bury his burgeoning arousal between her satin-soft thighs. Only the purple smudges beneath her eyes and the faint tremor of her mouth prevented him from joining her on the bed and making love to her until she accepted that marrying him was not just the right thing to do for their child, but for them too.

He drew the bedcovers over her as he saw that she was struggling to keep her eyes open. He had told himself that he hated her for hiding his son from him, but he had been lying, he thought bleakly. He did not understand why she had done what she had, and he was still furious with her, but she was the mother of his child and Mateo would always be a special link between them. Deep in his heart, and for reasons he chose not to define, he was *glad* he had a reason to make Lauren his wife—and he couldn't give a damn that she was not the aristocratic bride his family had expected him to choose.

'Trust me, *querida*,' he said with sudden urgency. 'I believe we can make our marriage work.'

Something in his voice brought tears to Lauren's eyes, and she turned her head slightly on the pillow so that he would not see them. 'I don't find it easy to trust,' she admitted thickly, losing the battle with the waves of sleep that were pulling her under.

Had something happened in her past which had caused her to value her independence so highly and made it hard for her to trust? Ramon brooded as he stood by the bed and looked down at her. There was so much he did not know about her, for during their affair he had deliberately not involved himself in her personal life. Maintaining that distance between them had made him feel he was in control of their relationship, but now she was to be his wife he could allow himself to lower his barriers. Perhaps, in time, he would be able to persuade her to lower hers.

CHAPTER SEVEN

THEY married two weeks later, in the private chapel in the grounds of the castle. The wedding was a low-key affair, with only close family and friends from the groom's side in attendance and no one at all from the bride's.

Ramon had asked Lauren if she wished to invite anyone from England, but she had decided against it, thinking to herself that it was going to be hard enough to fool his family that she was a joyous bride without having to maintain the charade for her friends. She *could* tell a few close colleagues from PGH the truth, she'd acknowledged. But stubborn pride made her want to hide the fact that her fairytale wedding to a handsome Spanish duke was in reality a marriage of convenience for the sake of their son.

'I don't want Mum and Alan to interrupt their cruise,' she had explained to Ramon when he had called her into his study to discuss the wedding arrangements.

'Who is Alan?' he'd queried.

'My stepfather. Mum married him two years ago, and this trip is a belated honeymoon.'

'What about your real father?' Ramon had hesitated when Lauren visibly tensed. 'Is he dead?'

Not that she was aware of, she'd thought bleakly. But she had not heard a word from her father since the day he had left, and she had no knowledge of his whereabouts. 'My parents are divorced, and I know Dad will be unable to come to Spain,' she'd told him, and had changed the subject before he could question her further.

And so, on a bright spring day, as the sun shone from a cloudless sky, Lauren arrived at the chapel alone and was escorted through the arched doorway by the chauffeur, Arturo.

Despite the warmth of the day she was icy cold, with tension cramping in the pit of her stomach as she began what seemed like an endless walk down the aisle under the curious gazes of the guests, her eyes fixed on the handsome, unsmiling man waiting at the altar. For a few seconds her nerve deserted her, and she was tempted to turn and flee. But then she caught sight of Matty, sitting on Cathy Morris's lap at the front of the church, and she took a deep breath. She would rather die than be parted from her son, and if she wanted to avoid a custody battle with Ramon she must marry him. It was as simple as that.

The skirt of her ivory silk wedding gown rustled as she walked. She had planned to wear the lilac suit she had worn to her mother's wedding two summers ago, but Ramon had insisted that the Velaquez bride must look the part, and had arranged for a top couturier to visit the castle and design her dress. The result was a deceptively simple sheath which emphasised her slender waist and the soft swell of her breasts, its neckline decorated with crystals that sparkled like teardrops in the sunlight which streamed through the chapel windows.

It was a dream dress, she had thought when she had stared at her reflection in the mirror back at the castle, while a maid had fussed around her, smoothing invisible creases from her skirt. But that was where the dream ended, and perhaps it was better this way. She wasn't going into this marriage with the weight of expectation that most brides carried, and so, she reasoned, she could not be disappointed.

She was too old to believe in fairytales anyway, she reminded herself as she halted beside Ramon and forced herself to meet his gaze. Something flared in his sherry-brown eyes as he stared down at her, but it was gone before she could define it as his thick lashes swept down and masked his expression.

Moments later the priest's voice rang out in the silent chapel.

'You're not going to faint, are you?' Ramon asked beneath his breath as they emerged from the cool church into bright sunshine and posed on the steps for photographs. 'You look very pale. Perhaps today is too much for you when you have only recently recovered your strength after the virus?' he said, frowning with concern.

She resembled a fragile wraith, he thought grimly, gripped by guilt because he knew he should have allowed her longer to recover from her illness. His impatience to make Lauren his wife was because he wanted to secure Mateo's future, he had told himself, but he knew that was not the whole truth. He wanted her with an urgency he had never felt for any other woman, and when she had walked down the aisle towards him in her bridal gown, her honey-blonde hair caught up in a loose knot so that stray tendrils framed her face, her clear grey eyes fixed steadily on him, his breath had hitched in his throat.

The pulse beating frantically at the base of her throat had been the only indication that she was nervous, and that betraying sign of her vulnerability had tugged on his emotions. He had blackmailed her into marriage by threatening to fight for custody of their son, and he'd half expected her to refuse to go through with the wedding at the last moment. But she had come to the chapel, to him, and when she had lifted her soft grey eyes to him and given him a tentative smile he had felt a curious ache around his heart.

'I'm fine,' Lauren assured him. Not for anything would she admit that the surge of emotions which had stormed through her when the priest had proclaimed them man and wife had made her feel light-headed. She glanced down at the bouquet of red roses she was holding and breathed in their exquisite fragrance.

'Thank you for the flowers,' she murmured shyly. 'They were a lovely surprise.' The butler had presented her with the bouquet as she had been about to leave the castle for the short journey to the chapel, informing her that they were from *el Duque*.

Ramon had sent her three dozen red roses the day after she had met him, with a note inviting her to dinner, she remembered. Her heart gave a little flip as she wondered if giving her roses on her wedding day held special significance for him.

'It would have looked strange if my bride had not carried flowers,' he said coolly.

Her smile did not falter. Theirs was a marriage

of practicality, not a fairytale, she reminded herself, and steeled her heart to ignore the haunting regret that things could not have been different.

The church service was followed by lunch at the castle. The kitchen staff had surpassed themselves, and the meal was spectacular, its finale being a beautifully iced five-tier wedding cake, which Ramon and his new bride cut together.

Lauren guessed that there was a certain amount of gossip among the guests concerning the fact that the Duque de Velaquez was marrying the mother of his son almost a year after the child had been born, and also that his new wife was not a member of the Spanish nobility. But no one mentioned such matters—at least, not to her face—and Ramon's relatives seemed happy to welcome her into the family.

Only one guest did not seem to share the delight of everyone else that the Duque had married. Throughout the lunch Lauren had been conscious of dark eyes subjecting her to a lengthy scrutiny, and on the few occasions when she had looked across the room her gaze had collided with the icy stare of a haughtily beautiful Spanish woman.

'Pilar is stunning, isn't she?' Ramon's sister Juanita murmured as she joined Lauren by the open French doors and followed her gaze out to the terrace, where Ramon was in deep conversation with the willowy, elegant woman whose mass of silky black curls fell halfway down her back.

'You've probably heard of her, or seen pictures of her at any rate,' Juanita continued. 'Pilar Fernandez is one of the world's top models. Only someone with her fantastic figure can wear a skirt that short,' she commented, with a rueful glance at Pilar's pure white suit, which contrasted so eye-catchingly with her exotic colouring.

'I suppose she'll concentrate on her modelling career now that—' Juanita halted abruptly, and looked so uncomfortable that Lauren's curiosity was aroused.

'Now that what?'

'Now that Ramon has married you,' Juanita muttered, clearly regretting that the subject of Pilar Fernandez had come up. 'It was kind of expected that they… Well, anyway,' she hurried on when she saw Lauren's face fall, 'Pilar is adored by top designers around the world, so I don't suppose she'll visit the castle as much as she used to.'

Ramon's sister's words were not reassuring, Lauren thought dismally. When Ramon had taken her to lunch in London he had dismissed his relationship with Pilar as nothing more than friendship, but clearly it had been more than that if there had been an expectation that he would choose *her* to be his wife.

It would have made sense for him to marry her, she brooded. Pilar was an aristocratic Spanish woman, from Ramon's elite social circle, elegant, sophisticated, and ideally suited to be a *duquesa*. Added to that, she was exquisitely beautiful. Doubts swamped Lauren with the force of a tsunami, drowning her common sense in a flood of insecurity. She could not compete with Pilar on any level, she thought dully as she tore her eyes from Ramon and his gorgeous 'friend' and looked down at the white gold wedding band that he had placed on her finger, next to the ostentatious ruby engagement ring that had been worn by previous generations of Velaquez brides.

Jealousy burned in her stomach when she saw the Spanish woman place her hand on Ramon's shoulder and lean close to him to whisper something in his ear. Suddenly she was fourteen, wearing her new dress and handing around mince pies at her parents' annual Christmas party. Her mum was rushing around, in her element as the busy hostess, but there was tension behind her smile when she came up to Lauren and asked if she had seen her father.

'I'll look for him,' she had promised, unconcerned. Her mother always flapped. But she had lugged the plate of mince pies all around the house, looking for Donny, and had found him at last—in the conservatory, with a blonde woman with a big bust who was the secretary of the golf club. Jean had been leaning close to her father, whispering something in his ear. And her dad had been smiling—just as Ramon was smiling at Pilar now.

'Hello, pet. What have you got there—mince pies?' Donny had walked towards her, laughing, blocking the view of Jean frantically pulling up the strap of her dress.

The awkward moment had passed, because Lauren hadn't understood why it was awkward, but a long time later, after her father had left his wife and daughter for an exotic dancer, she had recalled the incident and her mother had revealed that Jean had been one of Donny's many mistresses.

Lost in her memories, she stepped onto the terrace and wandered in the opposite direction from Ramon and his companion. She gave a start when someone spoke to her, and her heart sank when she looked up and met Pilar's haughty stare.

'Mateo is a charming child. Ramon is clearly very proud of him,' the Spanish woman commented in a distinctly cool tone.

'We both are,' Lauren replied politely, feeling uncomfortable beneath Pilar's intent scrutiny.

'Ramon married you to claim his son, of course.'

It was a statement rather than a question, and Lauren did not know what to say—it was the truth, after all, she thought dully.

Pilar's black eyes were as cold and hard as polished jet. 'How do you think you will cope with being a *duquesa*? I imagine that your life in England did not prepare you for joining the ranks of the Spanish nobility.'

Which, of course, was a pointed reminder that while Pilar had blue blood running through her aristocratic veins Lauren was a very ordinary English lawyer.

'I'm sure I'll manage,' she told the stunning model tightly.

Pilar shrugged her thin shoulders dismissively. 'Perhaps you will not be a *duquesa* for very long now that Ramon has his son,' she suggested softly, and walked away, leaving Lauren staring after her, shivering suddenly as a cloud covered the sun with a grey shadow.

The castle's huge master bedroom was dominated by a four-poster bed hung with velvet drapes. It was an enormous bed for one person—but perhaps Ramon did not sleep alone in it very often?

Lauren thought bleakly. Perhaps Pilar Fernandez had shared the bed with him during the eighteen months that they had been apart?

Stop it, she told herself angrily. She was making something out of nothing, just because Pilar had made that spiteful comment about Ramon not wanting her for his wife for very long.

Ramon was still downstairs, bidding farewell to the last guests, but in a few minutes he would join her. After her run-in with Pilar she had forced herself to rejoin the wedding celebrations, and had chatted and smiled until her jaw ached. But she had been conscious of his speculative glances, and when, in answer to his query, she had assured him that she was enjoying the day, his expression had been sardonic.

With a heavy sigh she walked through the connecting door into an adjoining room that he had explained was traditionally the Duquesa's bedroom. She did not know if Ramon and Pilar had once been lovers, and she did not want to know, she told herself fiercely. But she could not dismiss the sight of him standing close to the Spanish beauty. Their body language had spoken of an easy familiarity, and somehow the image of Ramon and Pilar had become muddled with the image of her father and Jean from the golf club, and she wondered if she was as blind now as she had been naïve at fourteen.

Her eyes felt scratchy, and when she caught sight of herself in the mirror she was suddenly desperate to get out of her wedding finery. The dress and the roses had all been part of an illusion, created by Ramon to fool everyone into believing that the Duque de Velaquez and his new bride were blissfully happy. But she knew the truth, and with trembling hands she tore off the dream dress and the fragile lacy bra she had worn beneath it. Searching through a drawer she dug out an over-sized cotton tee shirt that had been among her things sent over from England.

She was standing in front of the dressing table, brushing her hair, when Ramon walked in.

'Not quite what I had envisaged,' he drawled, as his eyes skimmed the baggy tee shirt that had faded to an unbecoming shade of sludge in the wash. 'Your choice of nightwear leaves much to be desired, *querida*. Although even *that* shapeless garment does not dampen my desire for you,' he added self-derisively, when she spun round to face him and he noted the faint outline of her nipples beneath her thin shirt.

He had discarded his tie and unfastened the top buttons of his shirt, and Lauren glimpsed his bronzed skin beneath. Leaning nonchalantly against the doorframe, his dark hair falling across his brow and his eyes gleaming with sensual heat, he was so sexy that she felt weak with longing— and she despised herself for it.

'What *did* you envisage?' she asked sharply. 'That you would stroll in here and demand your marital rights?'

His eyes narrowed on her tense face. His instincts had been right, he brooded. Something had upset her during the wedding party, and now she was as prickly and on edge as she had been when he had first seen her again in London.

'Not demand,' he countered quietly. 'I did not think I would need to. You are my wife, and I admit I had assumed we would spend our wedding night rediscovering the passion that has always burned between us.'

'I'm only your wife because you've decided that you want Matty to be your heir,' Lauren said stubbornly.

Ramon's jaw hardened. 'He is my son, and by definition also my heir. I would always have wanted him, but you did not give me the opportunity to be his father.'

'You had made it clear that I could only ever be your mistress. In your eyes I wasn't good enough for the grand Duque de Velaquez, and I believed you would feel the same way about my child.'

And that was the root of her resentment, Lauren acknowledged. She was only good enough for Ramon now because she had given him a son. Without Matty he would only have wanted her as his mistress. She was not a sophisticated Spanish aristocrat like Pilar Fernandez, but she was certainly not going to reveal her jealousy of the beautiful model to Ramon.

'I do not think of Mateo in terms of your child or my child. He is part of you and part of me, and we have married so that we can both care for our son, who we created together,' Ramon said, his accent suddenly very strong, and his words tugging on Lauren's emotions. 'I thought that for him we were going to do our best to build a relationship.'

'By having sex?' Lauren muttered scathingly.

He did not deny it. 'Sex is a start. It is where everything began, after all. I saw you across a crowded nightclub and I wanted you more than I had ever wanted any woman.' He paused, and then added softly, 'I still do. And I think, Lauren, although you seem determined to deny it, that you want me too.'

She could not meet his gaze, and stared at the floor through blurred eyes. Maybe he was right. Sex *was* a start. It had bound them together for the six months of their affair, and if she had not fallen pregnant who could say how long they would have stayed together? Ramon's desire for her had shown no sign of lessening. And it hadn't just been a physical act. There had been closeness, companionship—and for her, of course, love.

Was it fair to hold it against Ramon because he hadn't fallen in love with her? And was it fair to push him away and deny them what they both wanted because she was afraid that he would be a serial adulterer like her father? He had asked her to trust him, she remembered. He had no idea how hard that was for her, but if she wanted their marriage to stand a chance she was going to have to try.

'I'm not a beautiful blue-blooded aristocrat,' she mumbled, unable to forget Pilar.

'You are the most beautiful woman in the world to me,' Ramon said intently. 'And your blood could be bright green for all I care. You are the mother of my son.' He gave a rueful grimace. 'And the reason I have taken enough cold showers in the past few weeks to last me a lifetime.'

Her hair streamed down her back like a river of gold. There was wariness in her eyes, but something else too, that made him ache with his need to possess her.

'I have made a commitment to you, Lauren, and I want to put our differences aside and make our marriage work,' he said steadily. 'But you have to want that too—because it takes two to make a marriage.' He trapped her gaze, and she swallowed at the latent warmth in his golden eyes. 'Do you want to make our marriage a proper one?'

She could deny it and keep her pride, or she could accept a marriage that was not perfect, but which over time might grow and develop into a deeper relationship. It was her choice.

'Yes,' she whispered. A shiver of excitement ran down her spine at the hard glitter in his eyes.

'Then come here.'

The first step was the hardest, the second a little easier. And then he moved too, and met her halfway across the room, breathing hard as he snatched her into his arms. 'You looked so beautiful today, *querida*. But I have to admit that my main thought when I saw you in your wedding dress was how soon I could rip it off you.'

His sensual smile stole her breath. 'It gives me even greater pleasure to remove *this* monstrosity,' he growled, tugging the shirt over her head in one deft movement to reveal her firm breasts and slender waist, the tiny wisp of the lace thong hiding her femininity from him.

With a groan of need he swept her up and strode into the master bedroom, where he placed her on the bed and lowered his body onto the softness of hers, crushing her breasts against his chest as he claimed her mouth in a devastatingly sensual kiss. When he lifted his head, streaks of dull colour highlighted his magnificent cheekbones, and his hand was unsteady as he smoothed her hair back from her face.

'This was always how we communicated best,' he said roughly.

She did not reply, for really it was true. When they made love there was no need for words. They were perfect together. And that was why, in the heady days of their affair, she had fooled herself into believing that he was starting to care for her. She would not make the same mistake again, but she could not deny her need for him, and she tugged impatiently at his shirt buttons.

'Then make love to me,' she invited softly.

Their eyes locked and held for infinitesimal seconds, before he made a feral sound in his throat and captured her mouth again in a kiss that plundered her soul. She loved the way he kissed her, Lauren thought dazedly. Loved the hungry pressure of his lips on hers and the bold thrust of his tongue that erotically mimicked the act of making love to her. And then her mind ceased functioning as instinct took over, and she curled her arms around his neck and hugged him so tightly to her that she could feel the erratic thud of his heart beating in unison with her own.

She shivered with anticipation when he cupped her breasts in his palms. 'Gorgeous—and all mine,' he growled with intense satisfaction as he lifted his head to stare at the creamy mounds. He stroked his thumbs over her rose-pink nipples so that they swelled and pouted provocatively at him, and smiled at her soft whimpers of delight. 'You will find me a very possessive husband, *querida*,' he warned her, before he closed his mouth around one taut peak, and then its twin, and suckled her until she writhed beneath him and begged him never, *ever* to stop.

Ramon loved the way his cool English rose discarded all her inhibitions and became a wanton creature in his arms. Sex with Lauren had blown his mind from the start. No other woman had ever made him lose control the way he did with her, and he was already dangerously close to the edge. The long, leisurely seduction he had planned would have to wait until later, he thought self-derisively. Right now all he could think of was burying his swollen shaft deep inside her.

Lauren pressed back into the mattress and closed her eyes blissfully as Ramon trailed his mouth down from her breasts to her stomach, and then lower still. Her limbs felt boneless as the dull ache deep in her pelvis became an urgent throb of need, and she lifted her hips obligingly so that he could pull her knickers down. The molten heat between her thighs was evidence of her arousal, but Ramon seemed intent on giving her the maximum pleasure, and she gasped when he pushed her legs apart and dipped his dark head.

The feel of his tongue stroking up and down before probing gently made her tremble, and she tangled her fingers in his silky hair and sobbed his name when he closed his mouth around the sensitive nub of her clitoris. Everything was happening too fast; she was spinning out of control. But as the first spasms of her orgasm began to ripple he moved swiftly over her and entered her with one hard thrust that made her cry out.

'Did I hurt you?' he demanded tensely, his chest heaving as he fought for control.

'No.' She arched beneath him and wrapped her legs around his back, desperate for him to thrust again. 'Don't stop,' she breathed.

He suddenly seemed to realise that she was close to the edge, and slid his hands beneath her bottom to angle her so he could drive deeper into her.

It was hard and fast, both of them driven by a mindless urgency as he pumped into her with thrust after powerful thrust. Lauren clung to his shoulders, her eyes closed and her lips parted as she snatched air into her lungs. It couldn't last. The coiling sensation inside her was growing tighter and tighter. Her lashes flew open when he stopped moving, but before she could beg him to continue he altered their position and pushed her legs up so that they rested on his shoulders.

'Trust me, *querida*, it will be even better for you like this,' he promised.

And it was. He slammed into her and filled her to the hilt, each thrust so deep and intense that the pleasure was indescribable, impossible to with-stand.

'Ramon…' The coiling in her pelvis tightened one more notch, held for a few agonising seconds, and then snapped with explosive force, so that she bucked beneath him and clawed at his arms, utterly overwhelmed by the tidal wave of ecstasy that swept through her.

Her orgasm was mind-blowing, but a tiny part of her consciousness sensed that he was nearing his own nirvana, and she lifted her hips to meet his final savage thrust, heard the groan that was wrenched from his throat as his big body shud-dered with the force of his release.

It took a long time for Lauren to come back down, and she lay contentedly beneath Ramon, loving the feel of his warm, lax body pressing her into the mattress. At last he rolled off her, but immediately curved his arm around her and pulled her close.

'Tears, *querida*?' he asked roughly, brushing his fingers over her face and tracing the twin rivulets of moisture.

She could not tell him that in those moments of intense passion she had felt as though their souls as well as their bodies had merged as one.

'I just wish things had been different,' she whispered, imagining how it would be if he loved her. Perhaps he would murmur tender endearments in her ear, and she would be free to voice her love for him instead of hiding her feelings away.

Ramon frowned. 'Is being married to me so unbearable?' he demanded, feeling as though he had been kicked in the gut.

'Of course not. I accept that it was the right thing to do for Matty's sake.'

Why was her answer not as satisfactory as it should be? Their son *was* the only reason he had insisted on marriage, he reminded himself. He was pleased Lauren shared his belief that Mateo should grow up with both his parents, and the sizzling sexual chemistry between them was a bonus he intended to enjoy to the full.

'As you say, our son's needs are paramount. But tonight I intend to satisfy all *your* needs, as well as my own,' he growled, before lowering his head and slanting his mouth over hers to initiate a deep, sensual kiss that stirred the embers of their mutual desire.

Lauren might only have married him to keep her son, but she was a highly sensual woman. Her enjoyment of sex was uninhibited, and Ramon was unable to restrain a shudder of pleasure when she wrapped her fingers around his already thickening shaft.

He curled his hand possessively around her breast and lifted his head to stare down at her, pleased to see that her eyes were glazed with desire.

'Now you are my wife,' he murmured, unable to hide his satisfaction as he slid his hand between her legs and found that she was ready for him. 'And we have just proved that passion, together with a mutual desire to do the best for our son, are key elements to making our marriage work.' His voice roughened as he positioned himself over her. 'Especially passion—don't you agree, *querida*?'

She didn't, but she did not tell him. Instead she gave herself up to the exquisite pleasure only he could arouse in her. But later, when she lay listening to the rhythmic sound of his breathing, she wondered dully if she was destined to spend her life wanting more than he could give her.

CHAPTER EIGHT

'I've decided that we should have a honeymoon.'

Lauren opened her eyes to find Ramon leaning over her, looking disgustingly wide awake despite the fact that they had both had very little sleep the previous night.

'All right,' she mumbled, snuggling deeper under the sheet.

'Where would you like to go?'

She glanced at the clock, and firmly closed her eyes once more. 'Do we have to decide at seven o'clock in the morning?'

Ramon studied her, noting how the early-morning sunshine slanting through the blinds had turned her hair to pure gold. Her mouth was slightly swollen from his kisses, and recalling the taste of her and the feel of her soft lips parting beneath his he felt unbearably tempted to make love to her again. But she was clearly exhausted after their energetic wedding night, he thought, a feeling of tenderness tempering his hunger. Lauren was his wife now, and they had all the time in the world.

'We need to make plans so that I can mobilise the staff,' he told her.

Lauren gave up trying to sleep and rolled onto her back, her heart missing a beat when she met Ramon's warm sherry-gold gaze. 'You make it sound like a military operation. Why would the staff need to come on our honeymoon?'

'I have a villa in Barcelona. I thought we could take Mateo to the beaches there, and there are plenty of designer shops for you in the centre of the city. But there are no permanent staff at the villa, so we will need to take a cook and a butler, and other household staff—and Cathy, of course, for Mateo.'

'It's going to be quite a crowded honeymoon, then,' Lauren murmured, her initial excitement fading a little now that it sounded as though their stay at the villa would be as formal as life at the castle. 'To be honest, I think Matty is a bit young for the beach—we'll spend all our time trying to stop him eating the sand. And I really don't need to do any more shopping,' she added ruefully.

In the two weeks prior to the wedding Ramon had insisted on taking her shopping in Madrid several times, and her wardrobes were now bursting with couture clothes from all the top design houses.

'Couldn't we go somewhere on our own——just you, me and Matty? Do you remember that week-end we spent at a lodge in Scotland?' She smiled, remembering the trip they had made to the beauti-ful Scottish Highlands a month or so before she had found out that she was pregnant and their re-lationship had been blown apart. Ramon had been so relaxed that weekend, and had made love to her so tenderly in front of a blazing log fire that she had found herself falling ever deeper in love with him. 'It would be nice to go somewhere peaceful,' she said wistfully.

In the hectic run up to the wedding she had barely spent any time with him, and as the castle had been full of his various relatives they had had no chance to be alone.

Ramon frowned. 'Scotland will be cold at this time of year. But if it's mountains you want, I know of a place that is quiet and peaceful, with just the sound of a stream outside the house to disturb us. But it's not much—just a simple lodge. And there isn't room for any of the staff.'

'It sounds perfect,' Lauren assured him.

She knew many of her friends back in London would love to have an army of staff to take care of the cooking, housework and childcare, but she found the stiff formality of the castle rather stifling, and she didn't think she would ever get used to the maids bobbing a curtsy every time they saw the new Duquesa.

Ramon dropped a kiss on her mouth. 'That's settled, then. I'll instruct the staff to pack for us, and we'll leave in a couple of hours.'

'This is spectacular,' Lauren said in an awed voice a few hours later, as she climbed out of the four-by-four Ramon had driven from the castle up into the Cantabrian mountains. Below them was a lush green valley, with farmhouses dotted here and there, and orange and almond groves in full bloom. The stream that threaded through the valley was glinting like a silver ribbon in the sunshine. All around the wooden lodge where they were to stay were tall pine trees, and rising up behind them were the higher peaks of the mountains, capped with snow that sparkled pure white against the cornflower-blue sky.

The lodge was as basic as Ramon had said, but perfectly comfortable, with a large sitting room and kitchen, a main bedroom with a bathroom leading off it, and a smaller room where they would set up a travel cot for Matty.

They unpacked the car, and then Ramon took charge of his son while Lauren spread out a rug on the grass and opened the picnic hamper the castle cook had prepared for them.

'What a heavenly place,' she murmured, her eyes drawn to the towering mountains. 'Do you often come up here?'

Ramon carefully spooned some yogurt into Matty's mouth while the baby was distracted by playing with the car keys. 'Not as much as I would like. The responsibilities of running the company and the castle estate leave me with little free time, but when I was a boy I came up here most weekends, to hike or to fish in the mountain lakes.'

Lauren nodded. 'I can understand why. I love it here. And I love picnics. I always seem to eat twice as much when I'm out in the fresh air,' she said ruefully as she bit into another smoked salmon sandwich. 'I must admit I prefer meals like this much more than the formal dinners we have at the castle, with the butler and a dozen servants in attendance—even for just the two of us.'

Ramon frowned at her outburst. 'It has always been the tradition for the Duque and Duquesa to dine in the great hall. Even when my sisters and I were little my parents insisted that we should dress for dinner each evening, and we were expected to sit through five courses and make polite conversation without fidgeting or appearing bored.'

'Do you mean that you never ate pizza in front

of the TV? Or invited a few friends round and slung steaks on the barbecue?' Lauren said in astonishment.

'Certainly not. I was brought up always to be aware of my position and to act accordingly.'

She grimaced. 'No wonder you looked shocked when you caught me eating ice-cream out of the tub at your apartment in London—and when I ordered Chinese take-away and insisted that we picnicked on the living room floor. What on earth did you think of me?' she muttered, blushing at the memory.

She doubted Pilar Fernandez would experiment with chopsticks to eat sweet-and-sour chicken balls, and dribble the sauce down her chin. It emphasised yet again that she did not belong in Ramon's world, Lauren thought dismally.

'I thought you were fun,' he told her, smiling when she stared at him in surprise. 'I'd never met anyone like you before. You liked to do crazy things, like walking in the rain, and cooking bacon sandwiches after we had made love for hours and were starving.'

'Don't remind me,' she groaned.

'I could relax with you,' Ramon said quietly.

He hadn't realised how much he had enjoyed being with her until she had ended their affair and he had returned to Spain soon after, to help care for his dying father.

'I loved my parents, but my childhood *was* restrictive,' he admitted. 'I was brought up mainly by my governess, and I only saw my father for an hour each evening, when I was summoned to his study so that he could tell me about my ancestors, and the history of the castle, and instruct me on the duties I would one day take on when I became the Duque de Velaquez.'

'Did you want to be a *duque*?' Lauren asked curiously, trying to imagine him as a little boy, perhaps not many years older than Matty, being taught the responsibilities that lay ahead of him.

Ramon hesitated. It had been impressed on him by his father that a *duque* should be strong and in control of his emotions. From a young age he had understood that he must never cry—even when he had been thrown from his horse and had broken his arm. The lessons of his childhood were deeply ingrained, and he did not find it easy to confide his thoughts and feelings. But Lauren was his wife, and he realised that for their marriage to stand a chance he must now learn to open up a little.

Ramon's sudden grin reminded Lauren of the relaxed, carefree lover she'd had a passionate affair with eighteen—no, nineteen months ago. 'Actually, I wanted to be an astronaut,' he told her, laughing when she gave him a disbelieving look. 'I had a passion for science—especially physics, which I studied at university. After I completed my Masters degree I was offered the opportunity to study with the American Space Agency.'

Lauren's eyes widened. 'Did you take it? Why ever not?' she demanded when he shook his head.

'I couldn't,' he said with a shrug. 'I was the only son and heir of the Duque de Velaquez and I always knew that my life was to be at the castle, running the winery and the estate, and heading other Velaquez business interests.'

'So you sacrificed your dream for duty,' Lauren said slowly.

Ramon's strong sense of duty must have been ingrained in him as soon as he had been old enough to understand his family's noble heritage, she realised. And as the only son he had grown up knowing that he must marry—not necessarily for love. He must choose a woman with a similar noble pedigree to provide the next Velaquez heir.

It was small wonder he had never considered that an affair with his English mistress could ever lead to a deeper relationship. Even if he had begun to care for her, as she had hoped at the time, she understood now that he would not have put what he wanted before his duty to his family—he would never have allowed himself to fall in love with her.

'So, did you never come up here to the lodge with your father?' she asked curiously.

'No. I had various tutors. One of them enjoyed the outdoor life, and used to accompany me. I was educated at the castle because my father feared that I might make unsuitable friendships if I went to school,' Ramon explained when Lauren gave him a puzzled look. 'I only ever socialised with young people from a similar social standing to my own. It was only when I went to university that I realised how stifling my upbringing had been,' he admitted.

'I'm surprised your father agreed to you going to uni,' Lauren commented.

'It took me a long time to persuade him.' Ramon sighed heavily. 'And then I gave him good reason to regret his decision by falling madly in love with a topless model and announcing my intention to marry her.'

Lauren gave him a startled glance, feeling a sharp stab of jealousy that Ramon, whose heart was made of granite, could ever have been 'madly in love'.

'But I thought it was your duty to marry a woman from the Spanish nobility? What did you father say?'

'Naturally he was horrified, and tried to dissuade me. But I was eighteen, enjoying my first taste of freedom, and I was hell-bent on making Catalina my bride. That's when my father took action.' Ramon's smile faded as he remembered the pain he had felt when he had learned that he had been betrayed by the woman he had loved.

'He employed a private investigator, who discovered that Catalina had a lover. The lover was a drug addict, who needed money for his habit, and so Catalina came up with a plan to seduce the wet-behind-the-ears son of a wealthy *duque*, persuade him to marry her, and then make a mint from the divorce settlement. Armed with these facts, my father dragged me along to the hotel where he knew Catalina and her lover met in secret, and presented me with the two of them naked in bed together.'

'Ow,' Lauren murmured sympathetically. 'That can't have been a good moment.'

'There were plenty of others just as bad when the press got hold of the story. My humiliation was *very* public,' Ramon said dryly. 'I felt a fool—and, worse, I knew I had greatly disappointed my father. I soon got over Catalina, once I had seen that she was a mercenary slut, and in a way the whole sordid experience was good for me—because it taught me to be careful who I trusted. The Velaquez fortune is a powerful aphrodisiac for many women,' he drawled sardonically.

'Not for me,' Lauren told him firmly, horrified that he might have thought her to be a gold-digger when she had first met him. 'I was determined to train for a good career so that I could earn my own money and *never* be reliant on any man.'

'Your desire for independence is all very well, but you were wrong to keep my son a secret from me,' Ramon said harshly. 'You put what you wanted before the needs of our child.'

Lauren bit her lip. 'I've already explained that I didn't think you would want our baby when you'd just told me that you intended to marry an aristocratic bride. If I had known that you would love your child, regardless of his mother's social standing, I would have told you I was pregnant the night we broke up.'

The tense silence that fell between them was broken by Matty, who had grown bored with playing with the car keys and made a grab for the pot of yogurt, chuckling when yogurt flew through the air and landed on Ramon's shirt.

'You have to admit he's got a great aim,' his father commented as Lauren hastily took the yogurt pot from Matty, before he could spread its contents any further.

She glanced at Ramon, worried that he was annoyed with Matty, but Ramon laughed as he gathered him into his arms and lifted him high in the air, so that the baby squealed with delight.

'Even if you had told me, I don't think I would have had any concept of what having a child really meant. Nor would I have known that I could feel such a strength of love for my son,' he admitted in a low tone. 'Until I saw Mateo for the first time I had viewed having a child as a duty, to ensure the Velaquez name. I had never imagined what it would be like to be a father, to feel this absolute, overwhelming love for another human being and know that I would gladly give my life for his.'

Lauren swallowed the sudden lump in her throat, startled by the raw emotion in Ramon's voice. 'I know what you mean,' she said huskily. 'The first time I held him I was swamped by the most intense love for him, and everything else, including my career, suddenly seemed unimportant.'

Her eyes locked with Ramon's in a moment of shared parental pride for their son. Matty linked them together inextricably, she realised. For the first time since the wedding she felt a sense of calm acceptance that she had done the right thing by marrying Ramon, and that giving up her career was a small sacrifice when it meant that her baby would grow up with both his parents. But hearing

Ramon voice his love for Matty made her heart ache with longing that he would love her too.

'I always respected my father, but it was not until the last months of his life that I realised how much I loved him, and that he loved me,' Ramon admitted deeply. 'I was taught that men should be strong and hide their emotions. But my sisters' husbands are all excellent fathers, who do not believe it is a sign of weakness to show their love for their children. I want to be like them, but it is hard to change the habits that have been ingrained from childhood.' He hesitated. 'I need you to help me be a good father, Lauren.'

The note of uncertainty in his voice tugged on Lauren's heart. It took a strong man to admit he felt vulnerable, and she loved him even more for his honesty. Without pausing to think what he might make of her actions, she leaned towards him and pressed her mouth to his olive-skinned cheek. 'You're already doing brilliantly,' she told him softly. 'Parenting is all new to me too, but we can learn together.'

'That sounds good, *querida*,' Ramon murmured, turning his head so that his lips brushed over hers in a gentle kiss that stirred her soul.

There had been an unspoken promise in that kiss, of their unity in doing their best for their child, Lauren mused a little while later, when

Matty had fallen asleep and they'd carried him
back to the lodge. He did not stir when they laid
him in the travel cot, and as they crept from the
room and shut the door it suddenly struck her that
she and Ramon were alone—and this was their
honeymoon.

He must have read her mind, because he swept
her up into his arms and strode into the main bedroom, the hungry gleam in his eyes causing her
heart-rate to quicken. 'I think our son's idea of a
siesta is an excellent idea,' he stated, as he placed
her on the bed and began to unbutton his shirt.

'You're planning to go to sleep?' she asked him,
her voice emerging as a husky whisper as desire
flooded between her thighs.

'No. I'm planning to spend the next hour
making love to you,' he promised her, feeling a
gentle tug on his heart when he looked into her
eyes. He smiled at her quiver of delight when he
knelt above her and slid his hands beneath her tee
shirt to cup her bare breasts in his palms. Her skin
felt like satin beneath his fingertips, and with a
groan Ramon tugged her shirt over her head and
closed his mouth around one taut nipple and then
its twin.

He swiftly removed the rest of their clothes, the
urgency of his desire for her making him unchar-
acteristically clumsy. But Lauren did not mind

when she heard her cotton skirt rip. Her impatience matched his. She obligingly lifted her hips so that he could tug her knickers down, sighing with pleasure when he caressed her gently with his fingers before moving over her. He made love to her with tenderness as well as passion, each deep stroke taking her higher and higher, until with a cry she reached the pinnacle and fell back down, to be held safe in his arms.

They spent a glorious week in the mountains. Away from the responsibilities of being a *duque*, and running a multi-million-pound company, Ramon relaxed and became once more the charismatic, witty and amusing lover Lauren had fallen in love with in London almost two years before. It was a chance for them to rediscover the companionship they had once shared, and to focus on being parents to their son.

Lauren privately decided that they should escape the formality of the castle and come to the lodge for a least a few days every month.

The honeymoon had been a turning point in their relationship, she thought some weeks later, as she stepped into the elegant cream silk dress she had chosen to wear to the christening of Ramon's new nephews. Two weeks after they had married his sister Valentina had given birth to twin boys.

The christening service was to be held in the castle's private chapel and, knowing that Valentina was run off her feet now that she had four children, Lauren had offered to organise the reception.

Ramon emerged from the *en suite* bathroom, rubbing his hand over his newly shaven jaw. His steps slowed when he saw her, and his sensual smile evoked the familiar ache in her chest. 'You look beautiful, *mi corazón*.'

Her heart leapt at the discernible tenderness in his voice. It was not the first time he had called her 'his heart', but she must not get her hopes too high that he meant the endearment literally, she reminded herself. And yet in the weeks since their wedding she had felt that they *were* growing closer—mainly due, it was true, to their intensely passionate sex life. In bed they were dynamite— and they were in bed a lot, she acknowledged with a smile.

Ramon worked long hours, but this gave him the excuse to insist on early nights and lazy Sunday mornings, and of course there were numerous occasions when he took a coffee break that just happened to coincide with Matty's afternoon nap!

He might not love her, but he made love to her with a dedication that bordered on the obsessive. And, while their relationship was not exactly what she longed for, Lauren told herself that she was content with what she had. Ramon did not do anything lightly, and the dedicated playboy had transformed into an equally dedicated husband and father.

'I hope I haven't forgotten anything,' she murmured, running through a checklist of preparations in her mind. 'I want the party to be perfect for Valentina.'

'It will be perfect. I know you, *querida*,' Ramon said confidently. 'I've no doubt you have planned things with military precision—just as you organised the other three parties we have hosted since we got married.'

He had been impressed with the enthusiasm with which she had organised the events: two business dinners, and a reception for local dignitaries. Lauren had taken on her role of Duquesa with the same determination with which she approached every aspect of her life—especially motherhood.

But Ramon was aware that although she was devoted to Mateo she was sometimes bored with life at the castle. Most women would be happy to spend their time shopping with an unlimited credit card and visiting beauty parlours, but he had realised long ago that his wife was *not* most women, he thought wryly.

As he walked over to her he took a slim velvet box from his pocket. 'For you—because when I saw them they reminded me of the creaminess of your skin,' he murmured, pushing her hair over her shoulder so that he could fasten the string of pearls around her slender throat.

The necklace was exquisite, each pearl separated from the next by a tiny sparkling diamond which caught the light when Lauren turned her head. 'It's lovely, but you shouldn't keep buying me things,' she protested.

'Ah, but today is a special day,' he said, feeling the tremor that ran through her when he brushed his lips up her neck and lingered on the sensitive spot behind her ear. 'Today is the six-week anniversary of our wedding day. Did you think I had forgotten?' he queried softly, knowing that she was remembering that disastrous night in London, when she had wanted to celebrate the six-month anniversary of their affair.

'You said you didn't set great store by anniversaries,' she reminded him.

He smiled. 'But that was then, and this is now. Things have changed. I have changed, *querida*. And I think six weeks of marriage is worth celebrating, don't you?'

Her reply was lost beneath the hungry pressure of his mouth, and a long time later Lauren had to re-apply her lipstick before they hurried down to the great hall to greet the guests.

* * *

Later that afternoon the one hundred or so guests trooped back from the chapel to the castle after a beautiful christening service, to toast the birth of Valentina's newborn sons—Sancho and Tadeo.

They were adorable, Lauren mused. She had forgotten how tiny new babies were. Matty looked huge in comparison, and now that he was walking he just loved being part of the gang, getting up to mischief with his older cousins. His first birthday a few weeks ago had been a day of mixed emotions for both her and Ramon. She had shown him photos of Matty, some taken when he was a few hours old. But now, as she watched Ramon cradling one of his new nephews, she knew he was thinking of all the precious time he had missed in his own son's life.

Juanita had also been observing her brother, and now she strolled over to Lauren and Ramon. 'You're going to have to hurry up and have another baby, Lauren, if you want to catch us up,' she said cheerfully. 'Alissa has three, I have two, and now Valentina has four. It's definitely your turn next.'

There had been a lull in conversation among the guests assembled in the drawing room, and Juanita's words drew several curious glances in Lauren's direction. Conscious of Ramon's sudden intent scrutiny, she forced a smile. 'Mateo is only just over a year old, and for now I'm happy to enjoy him,' she said lightly.

The awkward moment passed, but the conversation with Juanita stuck in Lauren's mind for the rest of the afternoon. It *would* be nice to give Matty a little brother or sister, she acknowledged, and she knew, although they had not discussed the subject, that Ramon wanted more children. She sighed and wandered over to the window, watching Valentina pushing an enormous pram around the garden.

Why wasn't motherhood enough for her, as it was for Ramon's sisters? she asked herself dismally. She adored Matty, and loved being with him, but sometimes she was ashamed to admit that she longed to use her brain—and she missed her job. Perhaps when Matty was older she would be able to return to her career, she told herself. She did not want to work full-time; she loved being with her son too much to want to be away from him for any length of time. But one day she hoped to work part-time hours and regain a little of her independence.

Ramon had disappeared to take a phone call. It occurred to Lauren that he had been gone for ages, and she guessed the call was related to Velaquez Conglomerates. She hoped he would not have to rush off to the company's headquarters in Madrid, as he sometimes did, but even while she was wondering what was keeping him from the party he walked back into the drawing room and strode over to her, a forbidding expression on his face.

'Why didn't you just come out with it and tell Juanita that you are not planning on having any more children because your career is more important to you?' he demanded coldly.

One glance at his dark face warned Lauren that he was furious, but because of the presence of their guests he was fighting to control his temper.

'For that matter, why didn't you tell *me* that you're going to be working in London for one week a month—or is the welfare of our son so unimportant to you that you didn't bother to mention it?'

'Of course Matty is important to me,' she said sharply. 'He is the most important person in my life.' She frowned. 'How did you know…?'

'That you have been offered a job with a law firm in England?' Ramon finished for her. 'My mother asked to see the photo album of Mateo when he was first born, and I did not think you would mind if I took it out of your bedside drawer. But when I picked up the album I accidentally picked up this letter that was hidden beneath it.'

Lauren stared down at the letter he had thrust into her hand, and acknowledged that there was little point in denying its contents. 'I can explain—' she began, but Ramon cut her off.

'I'm sure you can,' he said sardonically. 'But it is Mateo who will want an explanation when he is a little older—as to why you have chosen to leave him for a week or more every month.'

'I have no intention of abandoning him,' she said tightly. 'And can I point out that *you* were away on business for three days last week, and you didn't worry too much about leaving Matty.'

'That's different,' he snapped. 'I am CEO of Velaquez Conglomerates, and sometimes business trips are unavoidable. But there is absolutely no need for *you* to work. You cannot deny that I give you everything you could possibly want or need.'

It was debatable whether she *needed* the numerous pieces of stunning jewellery Ramon had given her since their marriage, or the designer handbags and the wardrobe full of more beautiful clothes than she was ever likely to wear, Lauren thought heavily. She could not fault his generosity. But the fact he believed that material things mattered to her proved that he did not know her at all.

'I appreciate that it is not necessary for me to work,' she said quietly, 'but is it really so wrong to want to do the job I spent years training for? To wish for a little independence that will give me a sense of self-worth?'

'You and your damned independence,' Ramon growled impatiently. He did not understand what she wanted. He showered her with gifts in an attempt to make her happy, but hearing her bang on about wanting her independence felt like a slap in the face. 'Your place is here at the castle, as Mateo's mother and my wife. I will not allow you to leave our son for days at a time just so that you can follow some selfish whim.'

'You won't *allow*? Am I your prisoner, then, Ramon?' Lauren gave a bitter laugh, the happiness she had felt earlier in the day when he had given her the pearl necklace draining away.

A couple of guests had wandered into the drawing room, clearly intrigued by the sound of raised voices from their hosts.

'This is not a suitable time for private discussion,' Ramon ground out tensely—apparently forgetting that *he* had initiated the discussion, Lauren thought darkly.

'I think you should know—' she began, but he swung round and strode away before she could continue, leaving her staring angrily after him.

'Oh, dear! Do I sense trouble in paradise?'

Lauren stiffened at the sarcastic comment, and turned to see Pilar Fernandez step out from an alcove by the window. It was plain from her satisfied expression that the Spanish woman had overheard her spat with Ramon, but good manners prevented Lauren from accusing Pilar of eaves-dropping.

'Everything is fine,' she lied, and knew from the arch of Pilar's perfectly shaped eyebrows that the beautiful model did not believe her.

There was no escaping the fact that Pilar was absolutely stunning, she thought dismally as she made a lightning inspection of the other woman's scarlet silk dress, which fitted her fabulous figure like a second skin. She already knew the Fernandez family had been close friends of the Velaquez family for several generations, and Pilar had been at school with Valentina. Ramon had explained this when Lauren had questioned why Pilar had been included on the guest list for the christening party. Her father, Cortez, had suffered a stroke six months ago, and since then had become a recluse who never left the Fernandez home, Casa Madalena.

And so Pilar had attended the party alone—and had spent most of the day flirting with Ramon, Lauren brooded, recalling the sharp knives of jealousy that had stabbed her insides when she had watched the two of them laughing and chatting together.

'The trouble is that you do not understand a man like Ramon,' Pilar drawled.

Lauren's hold on her temper was close to snapping point. 'And I suppose you do?' she said tightly.

'Of course. We are from a similar social background. I am aware that Ramon takes his responsibilities as Duque seriously, and he requires a wife who is suited to the role of Duquesa.'

'Are you suggesting that *you* would make Ramon a better wife?' Lauren demanded, deciding that bluntness was the only way to deal with Pilar's sly insinuations.

The Spanish woman shrugged. 'Only Ramon can decide that.' She inspected her long, perfectly manicured fingernails and said obliquely, 'Do you know where he spends every Friday afternoon?'

'He drives out to inspect the vineyards with his estate manager.' Lauren frowned at the curious question. 'Why do you ask?'

'No reason.' Pilar's smile was reminiscent of a smug Cheshire cat's, but she sashayed gracefully back across the room before Lauren could ask her what she meant.

CHAPTER NINE

LAUREN was furious with Ramon, and avoided him for the rest of the party. By the time the last guests had departed she had a splitting headache, and was grateful when Cathy offered to give Matty his bath.

'Go and lie down in the quiet for a while. I always find that's the best remedy for a headache,' the nanny said kindly.

But when Lauren walked into the bedroom and found Ramon packing a suitcase her heart slammed against her ribs.

'You're going away?' she queried sharply.

'Something has come up at the Madrid office which needs my urgent attention.' Ramon glanced at her tense face and his jaw hardened.

He still felt bitterly angry with her, but seeing her looking so dejected made him want to pull her into his arms and make love to her. There were never any misunderstandings between them in bed. It was the once place they communicated perfectly.

'We'll talk when I get back,' he told her grimly.

'There's nothing to talk about,' she said flatly. 'I didn't take that job. I tried to tell you earlier, but you wouldn't listen.'

'But you were tempted to take it.'

'Yes, I *was* tempted.' She wasn't going to deny it. 'I worked for Pearson's before I went to PGH. I kept in contact with the MD there, and he emailed me out of the blue with an offer of some consultancy work. I let James Pearson know I was interested, but when he sent me more details and I realised I would have to be away from Matty I turned the offer down.'

Ramon slammed the lid of his suitcase shut. 'I don't know why you want to go back to work,' he said, his frustration tangible. 'I give you everything.'

Not the one thing she really wanted from him, Lauren thought dully. She had felt they were growing closer, but this argument proved that on an emotional level they were miles apart. She crossed her arms defensively in front of her. 'You wouldn't understand.'

'Then *make* me understand.' He caught hold of her shoulder and spun her round to face him. 'If our marriage is going to work, you have to trust me, Lauren.'

'It's not easy to trust when your trust has been broken,' she muttered. And yet if her relationship with Ramon was ever going to develop didn't she have to try?

'What happened?' he asked grimly. 'Did some guy let you down?' He raked his hand through his hair until it stood on end. 'I need some help here, because I can't work you out.'

'I told you my parents are divorced,' she said abruptly. 'They split up when I was fifteen—after my father left my mother for a twenty-year-old exotic dancer and disappeared to Brazil with her. He cut off all contact with me, and I haven't seen or heard from him since.'

Ramon heard the bitterness in her voice. Fifteen was such an impressionable age, and he sensed that she had been deeply hurt by her father's actions. 'That must have been tough,' he murmured. 'Did you have a good relationship with him before he left?'

'I adored him, and I thought he loved me—but presumably I meant nothing to him.' Lauren swallowed.

Even after all this time her father's desertion still hurt, and her sense of abandonment was as strong now as when she had been a teenager.

'The day he left was the worst day of my life,' she said bleakly. 'Dad was a barrister, and he worked long hours, but he always made time for me, and I was closer to him than to my mother. He taught me to play chess, pretended to like the music I liked, and most weekends he would drive me to gymkhanas so that I could compete on my pony.'

She stared down at her hands, ferociously blinking back her tears. 'He was my world, and I still can't believe he went away and left me. I've never even received a birthday card from him. It's as if I never existed to him—but I don't understand why. Even if he didn't want to be with Mum any more, why did he reject *me*?' She swallowed. 'I guess the truth is that he just didn't love me enough to want to keep in contact.'

'Did you have any idea that there were problems in your parents' marriage?' Ramon asked gently.

'No—they seemed perfectly happy to me. Mum was always busy with the WI and her bridge club—and, as I said, my father spent a lot of time at work. But they used to hold dinner parties and things, and people used to comment on what a strong marriage they had. I found out afterwards that it was all a façade,' she said heavily. 'Apparently Dad had been unfaithful for years, and had had dozens of affairs before he went off with his Brazilian pole-dancer. My mother put up with his infidelity because she was terrified that if she objected Dad would divorce her, and she would lose the house and the wealthy lifestyle she was used to. In the end that's what happened anyway. Unbeknownst to Mum, Dad had remortgaged the house, and he took all the money from their joint bank accounts before he jetted off to South America.'

'It must have been hard for your mother to suddenly become a single parent and have to support a teenage daughter. How did she manage?'

'She didn't.' Lauren sighed. 'The truth is Mum had some sort of breakdown. She had never had a job or earned her own money, you see. Her parents had been well-off, and she'd married my father straight after she left finishing school. But with no income to pay the mortgage the house had to be sold, and I had to leave my private school and transfer to the local comprehensive. Most of Mum's friends from the bridge club didn't want to know her any more, and she took to drowning her unhappiness in gin and tonic.'

'Dios!' Ramon frowned. He had always assumed that Lauren had enjoyed a comfortable middle-class upbringing, but the truth was clearly very different. 'What happened to you? You were little more than a child.'

'I had to get a job—well, three jobs actually—that fitted around going to school. I worked in a shop and did cleaning—anything to earn a bit of money to pay the rent on our flat and buy food. Luckily I was able to keep up with my school work, and I managed to get to university. I was determined to have a good career. You wonder why I want to retain some measure of independence?' she said fiercely. 'Well, the reason is that after what happened to my mother I vowed that I would *never* be reliant on another person, as Mum was on my father. When Dad left I was forced to grow up fast. I learned to get on with things, and now when problems occur I prefer to manage on my own rather than seek help from anyone.'

'Including bringing up your child on your own,' Ramon said slowly.

He had never really understood why Lauren had kept Mateo's birth a secret from him. It seemed such a cruel and vindictive thing to do, and that had puzzled him, because he knew she was not a cruel person. Her words gave him a sudden insight into why she had behaved as she had.

'Is that the reason you did not tell me you were pregnant?' he demanded.

She nodded. 'You regarded me only as your mistress, and I honestly believed you would not want our baby. But I was afraid you would feel an obligation towards your child, and I couldn't bear the thought of Matty growing up wondering why you did not love him, as I have wondered all these years why my father did not love me. I was scared at the prospect of being a single mother,' she admitted, looking away from him so that she missed the flare of anger in his eyes. 'But I had a good job, I knew I could cope, and so I decided to just get on with it.'

'You should not have had to cope alone,' Ramon said roughly, but his anger was directed solely at himself.

If he had been more open with Lauren during their affair, instead of allowing her to believe in his playboy reputation, she might have turned to him for help when she had needed it most, and he would not have lost the first precious months of his son's life.

From Ramon's tone it was clear that he had not been able to forgive her for keeping Matty from him, Lauren thought bleakly. She saw every day how deeply he loved his son, and she bitterly regretted the decision she had made when she had discovered that she was pregnant. But she couldn't change the past. It still hung between her and Ramon, and with a flash of despair she realised that it would always define their relationship.

'I thought that if you didn't know about Matty

you would be free to choose a bride better suited to being a *duquesa*.' She hesitated. 'Someone like Pilar. Juanita told me that everyone expected you to marry *her*,' she muttered when Ramon frowned.

'My sister has always allowed her tongue to run away with her,' he said tersely.

But, like a dog with a bone, Lauren found that she could not drop the subject. 'You can't deny that with her aristocratic background Pilar would have been an ideal wife and an ideal *duquesa*.'

Ramon shrugged. 'Perhaps so. But I didn't marry Pilar. I married you.'

He did not sound overjoyed by that fact, and Lauren was unaware that his mind was reeling as he tried to assimilate all that she had told him.

His jaw was tense when he picked up the suitcase and strode over to the door. 'To quote the words you used earlier—we just have to get on with it. I'll be back in a couple of days,' he told her curtly, and walked out of the room without a backward glance.

He phoned several times while he was away, but their conversations were stilted and entirely about Mateo.

'He's fearless,' Ramon said, laughing, when Lauren recounted one day how she had caught their daredevil son trying to climb out of his cot.

The mixture of pride and love in Ramon's voice tugged on her heart, and she felt a wistful longing that he would love her even half as much as he loved Matty.

He had said he would be home the following day, but when at midnight he hadn't arrived, or even called her, Lauren went to bed, made a half-hearted attempt to read a book, and finally buried her face in the pillows and wept silent tears.

He wasn't worth crying over, she told herself angrily, when she sat up to blow her nose. Her mother had cried constantly after her father had left, and she had vowed then that she would never allow any man to mean that much to her. But she had underestimated the power of love, she acknowledged wearily. She did not *want* to love Ramon, but her heart had a will of its own and it seemed hell-bent on self-destruction.

She was about to switch off the bedside lamp when the door suddenly opened and he walked in. Lauren's eyes flew to his face, and then to the bouquet of red roses he was holding. Her heart skittered in her chest.

'Thank you,' she murmured, when he silently handed the flowers to her. She buried her face in the velvety blooms and inhaled their exquisite fragrance. 'They're beautiful.'

She wished he would stop looking at her with

that curious, unfathomable expression in his eyes and say something. But when he did finally speak his words evoked a feeling of dread in the pit of her stomach.

'I need to discuss something with you.'

'I see.' She had hoped the roses were a peace offering, but maybe they were a prelude to him announcing that he was no longer prepared to try and make their marriage work.

He sat down on the bed, and her senses instantly flared when she breathed in the evocative scent of his cologne.

'I've been to Bilbao.'

She frowned. 'I thought you went to Madrid?'

'I did. I flew up to Bilbao this afternoon, instead of coming straight home.' Ramon suddenly smiled, the golden warmth of his sherry-brown eyes easing a little of Lauren's tension. 'I have some information that I think you'll find interesting.' He opened his briefcase and took out a booklet. 'This is the prospectus for the university in Bilbao. As I understand it you studied a different system of law to the system we have in Spain?'

Lauren nodded, confused as to where their conversation was leading. 'The UK follows the case law system, while Spain and most other European countries follow the continental system. The two are significantly different.'

'But you could study for a Spanish law degree at the university—perhaps on a part-time basis while Mateo is a baby. Once you qualify and he starts school I thought you could join the legal department of Velaquez Conglomerates, or look for a position with a Spanish law firm—whatever you prefer,' he said quietly, when Lauren stared at him in stunned silence.

'I don't understand. You were so against me going back to work,' she said faintly, trying to suppress a little spurt of excitement as she flicked through the university brochure.

'I want you to be happy,' Ramon said simply. It had taken two miserable days and nights away from her to acknowledge that Lauren's happiness was important to him.

Lauren bit her lip. 'It's a wonderful idea, and when Matty is a bit older I'll certainly consider it. But even studying part-time would mean leaving him for two or three days a week, and although Cathy is a great nanny—

'He won't be with Cathy,' Ramon interrupted her. 'I will look after him on the days that you are at university. I've already arranged for chief executives to take over many of my responsibilities at Velaquez Conglomerates. I've decided to take a back seat role in the company while Mateo is young. I will need to continue with my duties in running the estate, but I can arrange my work around your studies.'

He paused, his brows drawing together when he saw the shimmer of tears in her eyes. 'What's the matter, *querida*? I thought a modern-thinking woman like you would welcome the idea of sharing the care of our child equally?'

'I do,' she assured him. 'It's just that you've taken me by surprise. I didn't expect you to understand how I felt,' she added huskily.

Her smile tugged on Ramon's insides. 'You *should* expect it,' he said seriously. 'You are my wife, and it is my duty to try and make you happy.'

Lauren's heart sank a little at the word *duty*. She didn't want to be another of his responsibilities. It would be so much nicer if he wanted to make her happy because she was important to him, she thought, unaware of the faintly wistful expression in her eyes.

Ramon began to undo his shirt buttons, revealing his muscular chest, the golden satiny skin covered with a mass of fine dark hairs that arrowed down over his flat abdomen. Lauren's heart-rate quickened when he leaned close to her and slid his hand beneath her chin.

'I want our marriage to work, *querida*.' He paused for a heartbeat, and then added deeply,

'Not only for Mateo's sake. And to that end I am prepared to do whatever it takes.'

The first brush of his mouth over hers was nectar after two days without him, and she responded eagerly—like someone who had been lost in the desert and had suddenly discovered an oasis. She sighed with pleasure when he wrapped his arms around her and deepened the kiss, sliding his tongue into her mouth and exploring her with a sensual mastery that made her tremble.

He grinned as he stood up and removed the rest of his clothes with flattering speed. 'Anyway, I rather like the prospect of being a house-husband.'

Lauren's lips twitched at the idea of her macho husband transformed into a tamed pussy-cat. Her heart lifted. He might not love her, but he cared about her enough to want her to be happy, and that was more than she had ever dared hope for.

'You know that housewives are meant to be domestic goddesses in the kitchen and temptresses in the bedroom?' she murmured as she pulled him down on top of her. 'How does that work for house-husbands?'

'I've never been near a kitchen in my life,' Ramon confessed shamelessly, drawing the straps of her nightgown down her arms until her breasts spilled into his hands. 'But I'm a god in the bedroom, *querida*,' he promised, and proceeded to live up to his claim.

Was it tempting fate to think that life couldn't get more perfect? Lauren wondered a few weeks later, as she carried Matty up the steps of the swimming pool and wrapped a towel around his wet, wriggling body. Not that he needed a towel in the glorious Spanish sunshine that shone every day from a cloudless blue sky. But he *did* need sunscreen and a hat, she told him as she set him on his feet. He immediately toddled off across the grass, laughing gleefully when she gave chase.

The pool was set amid beautiful gardens, where the scent of jasmine and bougainvillaea filled the air. All around the castle stood the peaks of the Cantabrian Mountains, lush and green at their base, rising to silvery-grey bare rock towards the summits. Ramon was a keen hiker—yet another facet about him that Lauren had recently discovered—and with Matty secured in a baby carrier on his father's shoulders they went walking in the picturesque countryside most weekends.

Lauren was making the most of the summer, and treasured spending every day with Matty, but she was looking forward to starting her studies for a Spanish law degree in September. Ramon had driven her to Bilbao for her interview at the university, and afterwards they had spent a magical afternoon at the Guggenheim, world-famous for its collection of contemporary art. Then he had taken her to an exclusive five-star hotel, where they had enjoyed an even more magical night.

It was becoming harder and harder to hide her feelings for Ramon, she mused as she carried Matty back into the castle for his afternoon nap. 'At least I can tell *you* how much I love you,' she murmured to the tired little boy. He gave her a cheeky grin that as ever stole her heart, and she dropped a kiss on his cheek before tiptoeing out of the nursery.

The sound of Ramon's mobile phone greeted her when she walked into their bedroom. She frowned, realising that he must have left it behind, and after a moment's hesitation answered it. She explained to his PA that he was out in the vineyards and would not be back until early evening.

'I'll drive out to find him and give him his phone,' she assured Maria, when the PA went into a lengthy explanation about an urgent matter that required his immediate attention.

The Velaquez estate was huge, with miles of vineyards, but she guessed that Ramon would be at his estate manager's cottage. It was too far to walk in the hot afternoon sunshine, and so she slid behind the wheel of the sports car that was his latest gift to her, lowered the roof, and was soon speeding along the dusty tracks, with the warm breeze blowing through her hair.

It was a glorious feeling, and she couldn't help smiling. She hadn't thanked him properly for her car yet, but tonight she planned to wear a new sexy black negligee and show her appreciation by seducing him.

There was no sign of Ramon's Jeep outside the cottage. So he could be anywhere on the estate, she thought with a frown, as she brought her car to a halt and stared along the endless rows of vines. She sat for a few moments, wondering what to do, and was relieved when one of the estate workers ambled up the track.

'The boss not here,' the man told her in answer to her query. 'He used to come Fridays, but not now.'

Do you know where he spends every Friday afternoon?

Pilar Fernandez's curious question on the day of Valentina's twins' christening stole into Lauren's mind, and despite the hot sun beating down on her shoulderblades ice trickled down her spine.

There would be a perfectly reasonable explanation as to Ramon's whereabouts, she told herself firmly. She smiled at the worker. 'Do you know where *el Duque* is?

The man shrugged. 'Sometimes I see him drive along this track.'

'And the track leads where?' Lauren queried patiently.

'To Casa Madalena.'

All the joy went out of the day, and all the heat drained out of the sun. Lauren shivered and hugged her arms around herself, nausea churning in her stomach. So Ramon spent every Friday afternoon at the home of Pilar Fernandez, and had apparently done so for weeks—despite the fact that he had told her he visited the vineyards on Fridays. Why had he lied? she wondered, and gave a bitter laugh. It could only be because he did not want her to know about his regular visits to Pilar.

Her mother had told her that her father had pretended for years that he played squash at his sports club every Friday evening, when in fact he had been having an affair with his secretary.

Oh, God! Pain ripped through her, and she sagged against the car. She had been such a fool. When she had first met him Ramon had been a playboy who had never been faithful to any of his numerous mistresses for more than five minutes. He had married her because he wanted his son, and had bluntly admitted that she was not his ideal wife. But he had said that he wanted their marriage to work, and she had been so blinded by her love for him that she had seized on the nice things he had done for her as a sign that he was beginning to care for her.

Maybe he had encouraged her to accept a place at university in Bilbao so that she would be out of the way for a couple of days a week? Maybe he intended to invite Pilar to the castle, so that she could get to know Matty before he divorced *her* and married the aristocratic Spanish beauty who would make him a much more suitable bride?

Her overwrought imagination battled with her common sense. Ramon would have to be Superman to have the energy for an affair when he made love to *her* every night. But he had never given any indication that the wild passion they shared was anything more to him than simply good sex. He liked variety, she thought bleakly, remembering his reputation when she had first met him in London.

She climbed back into the car and stared along the track in the direction of the Fernandez home. She could go back to the castle and pretend that she did not know where Ramon really went on Fridays. Her mother had silently accepted her father's affairs for most of their marriage, and for the first time Lauren truly appreciated how much

Frances must have loved her husband to have tolerated a situation that was both humiliating and heartbreaking.

The worst thing was that she was actually tempted to do as her mother had done, she realised, wiping away her tears with shaking fingers. She loved Ramon so much that the thought of losing him lacerated her heart. But she could not live a lie. She had to know the truth.

So, heart pounding, she swung the car towards Casa Madalena.

CHAPTER TEN

THE sight of Ramon's Jeep parked in the courtyard of Pilar's home made Lauren grip the steering wheel so tightly that her knuckles whitened, and her legs felt weak as she walked up the front steps of the house.

'*Sí*, Señor Velaquez is here,' a uniformed butler confirmed when he came to the front door. 'He is in the pool house.'

It was obvious that the pool house was the new-looking glass-roofed building to one side of the main house. Lauren hurried across the courtyard, her heart racing with a mixture of anger and trepidation at the prospect of finding Ramon and Pilar together. No doubt the model would be wearing a skimpy bikini that showed off her stunning figure—or maybe she would be wearing nothing at all?

Swallowing the bile that had risen in her throat, Lauren pushed open the pool house door—and came to an abrupt halt as three startled faces stared at her.

Ramon and another man dressed in medical overalls were lifting a much older man, who could only be Cortez Fernandez, into a wheelchair.

Lauren glanced wildly around the poolside.

'Oh! I thought…Pilar…' She trailed to a halt as she met Ramon's narrowed gaze.

'Pilar is abroad on a modelling assignment. What *did* you think, Lauren?' he queried in a hard tone—and in that moment she knew that she had made a dreadful mistake.

'I thought…' She swallowed. 'I'm so sorry for my intrusion,' she mumbled to the elderly man, who was now sitting in the wheelchair. He shook his grey head and gave her a faint smile.

'It is I who should apologise, for stealing so much of Ramon's time,' he said in Spanish. 'I should have known that a new bride would want to be with her husband.'

The nurse wheeled Cortez away, and Lauren bit her lip as she watched Ramon stride towards her. His wet swim-shorts moulded his muscular thighs, and droplets of water clung to the whorls of dark hairs that covered his chest. The sight of his near naked body made Lauren feel weak for a very different reason.

He hadn't been cheating on her with Pilar. Relief overwhelmed her. But when he halted in front of her she sensed his anger and met his gaze warily.

'What did you expect to find when you rushed in here, Lauren?' he asked quietly, his voice suddenly sounding curiously bleak.

'Pilar said… Well, no, implied…' she corrected herself honestly. 'That you spent every Friday afternoon with her. I had put it out of my mind until today, when I went to the vineyard to give you your phone and discovered that you had lied about inspecting the estate, and in actual fact you came here every week.'

Ramon exhaled heavily. 'I do come every week. Cortez suffered a stroke six months ago, which left him unable to walk. His doctor suggested that he should swim regularly, to help strengthen the muscles in his legs, but the stroke left him feeling so depressed that he seemed to be giving up on life. Pilar asked for my help. I have always been good friends with Cortez, and I persuaded him to swim with me every week. But he is a proud man, who hates his disability, and when he asked me not to discuss his therapy with anyone I felt that I should respect his wish.'

Shame washed over Lauren and she dropped her gaze.

Ramon stared at her downbent head and did not know whether he wanted to kiss her or shake her. At this moment the latter seemed more tempting. He inhaled sharply. 'How *could* you think that I was in any way involved with Pilar?' he demanded savagely. 'I have never given you any reason to doubt my commitment to our marriage.'

He hadn't, Lauren admitted, guilt gnawing at her insides. It had been her and her wretched insecurity that had driven her to think the worst of him. 'Pilar deliberately put doubts in my mind,' she muttered. 'I think she hoped to make trouble between us.'

'She seems to have succeeded,' Ramon said tersely. He swung away from her and snatched up a towel. 'I can't help feeling that you are always going to punish me for your father's sins.'

Lauren gave him a startled look. 'What do you mean?'

'You don't trust me. And I'm not sure our marriage can survive without trust. Go back to the castle,' he ordered her roughly. 'I am too angry to talk to you right now. I usually play a game of chess with Cortez—and, in case you're wondering, the only female around will be his housekeeper, who is about ninety-three,' he finished sardonically.

Ramon did not return for dinner. A member of the castle staff informed Lauren that he had phoned to say he would be dining with Cortez Fernandez. Clearly he was still angry with her, and she could not blame him, she thought miserably as eleven p.m. came and went and he still had not come home. But his explosive tempers did not usually last for long, and, hopeful that they would soon make up after this latest row, she took a bath and afterwards anointed her skin with fragrant oil, before donning the daring black negligee she had bought to please him.

She owed him an apology, she acknowledged as she sat alone on the huge four-poster bed and studied the portrait of Matty that Ramon had commissioned for her. It now hung on the wall, so that it was the first thing she saw when she woke every morning. Even if he did not love her the way she loved him, he had proved over and over that he cared about her and respected her—and she had repaid him with doubt and mistrust that threatened to undermine their marriage.

Racked with guilt, she paced around the bedroom and finally pulled on her robe, intending to wait for him downstairs so that she could greet him when he came home—if he ever did, she thought painfully.

She was shocked to see a light spilling from beneath the door of his study, and after giving a hesitant knock she entered the room. He was sprawled on the sofa, his jacket and tie discarded in a heap on the floor, a glass of whisky in his hand—not the first glass he had drunk, she guessed, glancing at the half-empty bottle on the coffee table.

'I…I didn't realise you were back,' she said shakily, when he turned his head and stared at her through bloodshot eyes.

'Where else would I be, my darling wife?' He gave a sardonic laugh. 'Don't answer that. I'm sure your fertile imagination can come up with a dozen scenarios, featuring me sleeping with one of the many mistresses that you seem to think I have stashed away.'

'I am truly sorry that I doubted you,' Lauren said in a low tone. 'I had no reason to mistrust you. It was just…when you weren't at the vineyards, as I had expected, I thought about all the times my father must have lied to my mother—all his affairs that I knew nothing about when I was a child, but which broke her heart. For a few stupid minutes I thought that you were like him, but I know that you're not,' she choked, swallowing the tears that suddenly clogged her throat.

Ramon drained his glass and stood up, moving away from her to stand by the window that looked over the dark castle grounds and the shadowy mountains beyond.

'I should never have forced you to marry me,' he said abruptly. 'I can see now that it was a mistake.'

Fear greater than anything she had ever experienced caused the blood to drain from Lauren's face, and she felt hollow inside, as if her heart had been wrenched from her chest. 'You didn't force me—' she began, but Ramon shook his head.

'*Dios mio*, I threatened to fight for custody of our child. I gave you no choice but to be my wife. And now you feel trapped. You asked me once if you were my prisoner,' he said harshly. 'The answer is no, Lauren. I will not keep you here against your will any longer.'

She wished he would turn round, so that she could see his expression, because the dark, deadly serious tone in his voice was scaring her to death. 'I don't understand,' she whispered.

He shrugged. 'I am setting you free. Neither of us can be happy while you continue to be haunted by the way your father treated your mother. You are constantly waiting for me to let you down in some way, and ultimately that lack of trust will destroy our relationship.'

He paused, and then continued in the same emotionless voice. 'I will agree to a divorce, and to you taking Mateo back to England. All I ask is that you allow me to buy a house for the two of you, and for your agreement that I can visit him often.'

She was so shocked by his stark announcement that she could not speak—couldn't think. The agonising pain, as if her heart was being crushed in a vice, made it difficult to breathe.

'I don't want a divorce,' she stammered. 'I would never take Matty away from here—from the castle, and his family, and *you*. I know how much you love him.'

She broke off when Ramon turned to face her, and the stark wretchedness in his eyes made her want to weep. She knew how much it must have cost him to offer her custody of Matty, to allow her to take his son away. He thought she wanted her freedom, but what she really wanted, *needed* to do was tell him honestly how she felt about him. She had been a coward for far too long, and had allowed her father's behaviour to colour her judgement of Ramon, but what they shared was too special to lose.

Courage was hard to find as she stared at the tall, handsome man who was her world. His jaw was tense, his skin drawn tight over his slashing cheekbones. She wished he would smile and hold her, kiss her hair as he did every night as she fell asleep in his arms.

She took a deep breath.

'I don't feel trapped. I want to remain married to you because...I love you.'

The silence was so intense that Lauren could hear the ragged sound of her breathing. There was no reaction on his hard face, and his thick lashes hid the expression in his eyes.

'Some *love*,' he said scathingly at last. 'You say the words, Lauren, but you did not show it today, when you believed that I was having an affair with Pilar.'

Feeling as though she were dying inside, Lauren stared at the floor, willing her tears not to fall until she was alone and could deal with his rejection in private. She did not see him move, and flinched when he slid his hand beneath her chin and tilted her face to his.

'True love—the kind that lasts for ever—is profound and loving, passionate and tender,' he said deeply. 'It is about trust and forgiveness, friendship, and an abiding affection that transcends all life's problems and disappointments and brings the greatest joy.' Ramon paused and stared into her grey eyes, feeling his heart contract when he saw the shimmer of her tears. 'At least that is the love I feel for you, *mi corazón.*'

It was too much to take in. He had defined the meaning of love so beautifully that she could not hold back her tears. She must have misunderstood. He could not mean that he felt that wealth of emotion for *her*, she thought desperately. But the golden gleam in his sherry-brown gaze burned into her soul, and to her amazement love blazed in his eyes.

'You…you love me?' She was a lawyer, and she always verified her facts.

'With all my heart, *mi preciosa.*'

The raw emotion in his voice touched her even more than the words, and she realised that she was not the only one who was shaking. Questions swirled in her head.

'Why didn't you say?' she whispered, still finding it impossible to believe.

He gave a rueful smile and stroked her hair back from her face with an unsteady hand. 'At first I did not know,' he admitted huskily. 'All I knew was that I fancied you like hell and wanted you in my bed. To my annoyance, I missed you when you weren't around. But I think even then, during our affair, I knew you were special,' he said slowly.

'You know what happened the one and only other time I fell in love. My heart soon mended after Catalina, but I felt ashamed that I had disappointed my father, and I was determined to one day marry a woman from my own social circle of whom he would approve. My experience with Catalina made me wary of trusting my judgement of women, so when I met you and realised I wanted more than a casual affair with you I reminded myself that I could never allow our relationship to develop.

'I was furious when I discovered that you had kept my son a secret from me, but I was secretly glad that it gave me the opportunity to make you my wife,' he admitted. 'I kidded myself that I only wanted to marry you for Mateo's sake. When you walked towards me in the church, looking like an angel, I knew that you had stolen my heart irrevocably and for ever.

'Don't cry, *mi corazón*,' he said softly, brushing his lips over her damp cheeks and tasting her tears. 'Don't you want me to love you?'

'I want it more than anything in the world, and I always have—because I fell in love with you about five minutes after I met you,' she told him fiercely. 'I'm crying because I was so unsure of you, and of the happiness that we seemed to have. I wish you had told me how you felt.'

'You wouldn't have believed me,' he said gently. 'You had to learn to trust me first. I tried to show you how much you meant to me.'

'By giving me things,' Lauren murmured, suddenly understanding that the jewellery and other presents he had showered her with had been his way of trying to teach her that he loved her. 'Oh, Ramon.' She stared at his beautiful sculpted face and ached with love for him. 'You wouldn't really have agreed to a divorce, would you?' she asked, a little tremor of uncertainty still in her voice.

'You must be joking.' He smiled suddenly, and snatched her into his arms as the restraint he had imposed on himself crumbled beneath his urgent need to hold her close. 'Even as I said it I was frantically backtracking and planning how I could persuade you to stay with me. I never want to let you go, *querida*,' he said, suddenly serious again. 'But I blackmailed you into marrying me. You have to choose whether or not you *want* to be my wife.'

Joy unfurled in Lauren's heart and radiated out, until every cell and nerve-ending in her body overflowed with happiness. 'I choose you—and I want to stay with you as your wife, friend and lover until I die.' She untied the belt of her robe and shrugged it from her shoulders, heat sizzling in her blood when Ramon studied the very daring black lace negligee with rampant appreciation in his eyes. 'But I won't object if you want to persuade me a *little*,' she invited in a sultry tone.

The sight of her creamy breasts spilling out of her sexy nightgown was too much for Ramon, and with a groan he lowered his head and captured her mouth with a sensual mastery that elicited her urgent response. She was on fire for him instantly, and curled her arms around his neck as she pressed her body up against his hard thighs.

He was breathing hard when he finally lifted his lips from hers. 'I have something for you,' he told her raggedly.

She smiled and stroked her hand over the distinct bulge beneath his trousers. 'I know.'

'Witch.' He eased away from her, strode over to his desk, and retrieved a small box from a drawer. 'I've wanted to give you this for weeks, but the time never seemed right.' He paused, and then added a shade bleakly, 'And I wasn't sure you wanted my love for you that this ring represents.'

He opened the box, and Lauren caught her breath as she stared at the exquisite sparkling circlet of diamonds set in white gold. 'One day our son can give this "monstrosity" to *his* fiancée,' Ramon told her, his eyes glinting with amusement as he tugged the enormous ruby engagement ring that she so disliked from her finger, and replaced it with the band of diamonds. 'This ring is for eternity, *mi amor,* just like my love for you.'

There were not words to express the depth of her love for him, but he seemed to understand, and kissed away her tears before he swept her up and carried her out of the study. The speed with which he took the stairs was an indication of his fierce need to make love to her. He dropped her onto the bed and removed the wisp of tantalising black lace, his eyes burning with desire as he swiftly stripped out of his clothes and positioned himself between her satin-soft thighs.

'I can't wait, *tesoro*,' he murmured, as he caressed her with gentle fingers and found her wet and ready for him. But he forced himself to be patient, and reached into the bedside drawer for a protective sheath, giving her a puzzled look when she took it from him.

'I think it's time I caught up with your sisters,' she said softly. 'Matty needs a little brother or sister, and this time I want you to be involved from conception to birth—concentrating very much on conception,' she added with a blissful sigh, when his patience snapped and he surged into her.

'Are you sure you want another baby when you are about to start studying?'

'I can study while I'm pregnant—and one day when our children are older I'd like to resume my career. I have everything I could ever want,' she reassured him softly, 'You, Matty, and hopefully we'll be blessed with another baby. But, more important than anything, I have your love—as you have mine.'

'For ever,' Ramon vowed fervently. And there was no need for further words as he showed her with his body the love that filled his heart.

* * * * *